Sosa Gang

Romell Tukes

**Lock Down Publications and Ca$h
Presents**

Sosa Gang

A Novel by *Romell Tukes*

Romell Tukes

Lock Down Publications
Po Box 944
Stockbridge, Ga 30281

Visit our website @
www.lockdownpublications.com

Copyright 2023 by Romell Tukes
Sosa Gang

Lock Down Publications
Like our page on Facebook: Lock Down Publications @
www.facebook.com/lockdownpublications.ldp
Book interior design by: **Shawn Walker**
Edited by: **Mia Rucker**

Sosa Gang

Stay Connected with Us!

Text **LOCKDOWN** to 22828 to stay up-to-date with new releases, sneak peaks, contests and more...
Thank you.

Submission Guideline.

Submit the first three chapters of your completed manuscript to ldpsubmissions@gmail.com, subject line: Your book's title. The manuscript must be in a .doc file and sent as an attachment. Document should be in Times New Roman, double spaced and in size 12 font. Also, provide your synopsis and full contact information. If sending multiple submissions, they must each be in a separate email.

Have a story but no way to send it electronically? You can still submit to LDP/Ca$h Presents. Send in the first three chapters, written or typed, of your completed manuscript to:

LDP: Submissions Dept
Po Box 944
Stockbridge, Ga 30281

DO NOT send original manuscript. Must be a duplicate.

Provide your synopsis and a cover letter containing your full contact information.

Thanks for considering LDP and Ca$h Presents.

Acknowledgements

First and foremost, all praises are due to Allah. Much love to all the readers rocking with me, I'm the HOV of the pen game, it's always a movie. Shout out Yonkas and Peeky, NY CB, Moreno, SG, YB, Lingo, Baby James, Spayhoa, Bagner, Brisco, Smurf, and Chino. My Brooklyn guys, OG Chuck, Tim Dog, Lil YB, Tails, and Gunny. Shout out the Bronx, S.I. my bro Dex, shout out to Philly, OG Munchie, Big C, Lezz, Dama, Banger, and Big Beast. Shout out LDP and Ca$h, the game is ours. Life is what you make it, but there is always a blessing in a curse. Shout to everybody who stood tall in the state and FEDS, respect and never degrade your morals. Stand strong on what you believe in. Enjoy this book and thank you for the support, it will always be worth your while.

Romell Tukes

Sosa Gang

Prologue

In the rough streets of Philly, there is a new crew on the rise, called Sosa Gang, with soldiers from all over the city.

The main leader, Sosa, is a young man with big dreams to put his niggas on to a big bag and see them rich forever.

When Sosa lands a plug, his life changes over night, and so do his boys, Twin, Lez, and Lil Hak.

The gang name starts to ring all over the city of brotherly love, but another crew ain't liking it, which turns the city into a horror film.

The Outlaws are the most dangerous crew in Philly, besides Sosa Gang, but the two had a long ongoing beef for years. With money involved, things get serious, and the two crews will bump heads like bull horns.

Crispy and Sin run the Outlaws, but will they let some young bulls take everything they've been working so hard to build?

The D.C crew is the laid-back clique, in their own lane, forced to pick a side or become fresh food.

The city violence will spark every law enforcement agency to look into them, but there are a lot of secrets and hidden agendas in each crew. Who could trust who, when everybody is out for blood, power, and revenge?

Romell Tukes

Sosa Gang

Chapter 1

Southwest Philly
Two Years Prior

Sosa called a meeting with his close friends in back of Bartram High School on the football field, where he used to play football before he recently graduated.

Sosa looked around at Lil Hak, who was from Southwest just like him. Lez Woh was from West Philly and his best friend, Twin, was from South Philly. For years, the group had been thick like brothers, even though they were all from different parts of the city, besides Sosa and Lil Hak.

The crew called themselves Sosa Gang, since the elementary days, when they all met each other on the playground. Ever since then, it had been love.

"Why you call us out here for, bro? I was fucking the shit outta wifey, and you know how crazy Foxy gets when I'm gone too long," Lez said, making everybody laugh because they all knew Foxy. She was considered one of the guys.

"Nah, this some real shit, bull. I've been doing a lot of thinking. Since I'm done with school, I figure it's time we all try to get some money," Sosa said, seeing everybody nod.

"Doing what though?" Lil Hak asked, the short tempered one out the bunch.

"I am speaking to Block tonight. Then, after that, the decision will be in my father's hands," Sosa told them, hoping it meant the world. But his dad, Barry, wanted Sosa to head straight to college because Sosa was way too smart to follow his and Block's footsteps in the game.

"You think Barry is gonna be with that, cuz?" Twin asked, knowing Sosa's dad for years because he always came down to Twin's pop's mosque.

"It's a try, bro. But if he says yeah, then, man, we gonna be on," Sosa cheered.

"What about the ops?" Lil Hak said.

"The Outlaws?" Sosa asked.

"Yeah, and the D.C. crew," Twin added.

"They can either get down or lay down, cuz niggas know the motto. We got numbers and Blocks. When they start seeing how niggas getting money, they ain't gonna have no choice but to get wit us or starve." Sosa made a point to them.

"Let's be real, scrap, Sin and Crispy ain't going for that shit. We already beefing with them niggas and we not even getting money yet," Lez said.

"So, let's set an example to let them know we run the city," Twin said.

"Dem niggas put Yeezus in the hospital last night. Crispy brother did it, I heard," Lez said, hating all the Outlaw niggas.

"Me and Twin gonna take care of that today. But I just need to know we are all together and on the same page, bull." Sosa addressed everybody because he needed the whole gang to be in on trying to lock down the city's drug trade, which was crazy.

"I'm wit it," Lil Hak spoke up first.

"Of course, I'm down till death do us part, bull. Facts," Twin added.

"I know we gonna have some big issues, but I'm for the gang. But we need to have structure and loyalty within our own hoods because we growing every day. I be hearing little niggas everywhere I go screaming out Sosa Gang," Les said.

"So, we are all good. I think the only niggas we have to worry about is the Outlaws because them D.C. crew niggas, focused on getting to Wayne and Roddy, ain't worried about us, cuz," Sosa added, as Twin agreed.

"We gotta get rid of Sin and Crispy. The Outlaws have been going at it with us for years, just because of who we are," Lil Hak said.

"In due time, bro. Them niggas move like the Mob, bull. And they playing for keeps," Sosa said.

"So are we," Lez shot back.

"Facts. That's why we gonna send a message to them fuck niggas tonight," Sosa said, as Twin's cell phone went off.

12

Twin answered his phone, going back and forth with someone on the other line. Everybody wondered what was going on because Twin looked sad and mad.

"You good, cuz?" Lil Hak said, puffing on a Newport cigarette.

"Nah, bro. Yeezus ain't gonna make it. He died in his coma, like ten minutes ago, his brother told me," said Twin, sounding disappointed because Yeezus was a soldier from South Philly.

"This shit ain't right, bull," Lez said, who was close to Yeezus also.

"They killed two of ours this year already, and plus Yeezus." Lil Hak was furious.

"We gonna get back scrap," Twin was sure about that. He already had a plan in mind.

"Gee just wrote me a letter. He in a new spot. I'ma give y'all his address so everybody can write and send him some bread," Lez said, changing the subject because the whole gang was in their bag about Yeezus' death.

"Twin, tonight when the sun goes down, meet me at my crib and I am with y'all, after I speak with the fam about getting to this paper," Sosa said, embracing everybody before he called an Uber to his crib.

Sosa, whose real name was Sean P. Garrison, was 18 years old and had a bright future ahead of himself. He was tall, with brown skin, handsome, with a well-defined body and good wavy hair. The girls loved Sosa, especially his calm and cool demeanor.

Being the leader of Sosa Gang came with a lot, but he kept a low profile. Nobody really knew him or his real name. Most of the time he would give people a false nickname, so they wouldn't assume he was the Sosa dude from Sosa Gang that everybody talked about.

When they first started the gang, nobody knew the crew would spread like wildfire throughout the whole city. Sosa knew if he could feed his gang, then they all would become millionaires overnight. His brother was one of the biggest bricklayers in town, but the real boss was their dad, Barry, who controlled a lot of the drugs going in and out of Philly.

If Sosa's plan all came together, he knew his people would be on for life. They wouldn't have to worry about being fucked up and broke in the hood, looking for come up. Sosa's Uber arrived as he walked up the block, and he went to Sharon Hill to prepare for tonight.

***

Sharon Hill, Philly
Hours Later

Twin waited in his car up the block from Sosa's crib, which was in a nice middle class area, a lot different from South Philly, where he was from. Twin was the same age as Sosa, with no feelings towards life, besides his gang and religion.

His dad Imam Ahmad was one of the most respectable Imam in the city. Twin practiced his Islamic religion, even while being locked into the streets.

Wilson Projects was one of the worst hoods in South Philly, but Twin loved it, and everybody loved him down there.

Twin had a twin sister named Traina. They looked just alike. Every boy in South Philly wanted a piece of Traina's thick, curvy body, but they were scared of Twin.

Sosa creeped up the block, wearing an all-black sweat suit, with a hoodie, as if he was about to rob some liquor store.

"You ready, bull?" Sosa asked, climbing into the passenger seat of Twin's hooptie.

"Yeah, but you're taking this killing shit to the next level," Twin said, pulling off while Sosa put on the OJ gloves.

"Nope, I'm just cautious, no DNA, no witnesses."

"Facts. Did you speak to Block?"

"No, he wasn't there with my sister. She was doing her school-work and all over social media," Sosa stated.

"Zarhya's butt is smart as hell. What she got left of school, two years?"

14

"Yeah, two years left of high school. I can't believe she went to a private school," Sosa said, as Twin drove through South Philly.

"This nigga Crispy's brother be fucking with this cute, little stripper bitch named Sandy, I heard. And I got the drop on them, thanks to Zels."

"Where is Zels? I fucks with the young bull. He just extra wild," Sosa said.

"He wit dem little niggas in Bartram Projects, trying to rob anything," Twin laughed.

"This is why we need the drugs, so niggas ain't gotta do that dumb shit. Feel me?"

"Facts. I agree 100%, bruh," Twin said, pulling up to the building Crispy's brother, Swank, was supposed to be at tonight.

"I'm trying to be pushing a Maserati truck in a few months," Sosa joked, but was also real serious.

"I need me one of them Benz Coupes," Twin said, looking at the building Swank should be in.

"Let's go inside, but let's make it quick. People ass nosy around here. But how we gonna get inside?" Sosa forgot about getting inside.

"I got this," Twin said, hopping out of the car.

Romell Tukes

Chapter 2

South Philly

Swank looked at Sandy like she'd lost her fucking mind as Sandy walked back into the living room.

Swank was Crispy's brother and down with the Outlaw crew, who had Philly on lock, moving weight and killing whoever got in their way.

"Let me get this shit right, Sandy. You called my phone to chill, knowing you got your damn period today?" Swank was pissed off because he only came through to fuck her phat ass. She had some wet pussy.

"Oh, so you only came by to fuck me, now?" She got hyped.

"Yeah you're a dancer, Sandy. This shit is more so like a business agreement," Swank said with a chuckle, but Sandy wasn't even smiling.

"Nigga, you wasn't saying that when you was eating my ass."

"That was one time, bitch."

"Well, how about the two times I ate your ass, and you said you loved me," Sandy said smiling.

"Bitch, I told you to never bring that shit up." Swank got heated because she promised him that would be their little secret.

"I'm sorry, daddy. I know what you want." Sandy took a sip of water and got between his knees to give him a crazy blow job. Sandy had a talent with her mouth, she was one of the best in South Philly.

Neither one of them heard footsteps creep into the living room.

"Party over here," Twin said, scaring both of them.

"Oh my god," Sandy yelled, looking at the guns.

Swank was frightened when he saw Twin, but he had no clue who the other man was next to him, dressed in all black.

"Swank, the nigga you and all your boys jumped outside of the bar ain't make it, and we here to collect, bull," said Twin.

"Man, I ain't have shit to do with that. I swear to Allah, bro," Swank lied.

"One thing I hate more than a bitch nigga is someone who would lie on Allah," Twin got real upset as he clutched the trigger.

"Crispy sent that hit on Yeezus, not me, bro. come on, cuz. I went to school with you, Twin. I would never cross your gang like that. Everybody know how y'all coming." Swank tried everything to talk his way out of it.

"Swank, you're not getting out of this. And, Sandy, if you move one more inch, I'll blow your fucking brains out," Twin said, as Sosa just stood there, ready to get it over with. But Twin was enjoying the show.

"Y'all Sosa Gang niggas always on some bullshit," Sandy mumbled.

"What, bitch?" Twin asked her.

"Nothing. Can y'all just kill his dirty dick ass and leave me. I got a career," Sandy boasted.

"Bitch, you're a stripper. Can y'all kill this bitch first?" Swank said.

Sosa couldn't help but laugh at the two.

"We have to slide on," Sosa said, feeling his cell phone vibrate.

"I'ight," Twin said.

Boc. Boc. Boc.

Bloc. Bloc. Bloc.

Twin hit Swank in his face three times. Sandy jumped up, thinking about running, until Sosa hit her in the breast three times, killing her.

***

Sharon Hill, Philly

Sosa got dropped back off at his pop's crib to see Block and his dad were both there. Block didn't live there. He had his own crib with Maggia, who was Block's girlfriend and also a bartender in the night life.

"What's up, bro," Block said. He was in the kitchen, making a plate of food from last night's leftovers that their dad's new girlfriend made.

"Chilling, but I been meaning to link up with you."

"Why are you dressed like a black ninja," Block said, laughing at him.

"You wondering about the wrong shit." Sosa took a seat on a kitchen stool.

"Daddy's bitch looks better than mine, and she a lawyer or paralegal. She fire. I'm jealous. I know she is wearing his old ass out," Block said, but Sosa wasn't trying to hear none of that shit.

"I'm trying to get on," Sosa said.

"What the fuck you talking about?" Block took a bite of roast beef, before placing it in the microwave to warm up.

"Nigga, I want to get into the family business." Sosa saw Block turn around wit his big diamond chain worth $120,000.

"You wanna sell drugs?" Block laughed in his face because Sosa had always been the school nigga with a promising future in somebody's college.

"I'm not joking."

"Your little crew must've put you up to this." Block knew of the Sosa Gang little crew running the streets wild, but he had no clue who Sosa was. Everybody knew him by his real name, Sean. Only a few knew him as Sosa.

"This is my idea, and if you don't help me, I'll find someone else," Sosa said, seeing Block get serious.

"Sean, this ain't no game. You not really a street nigga. You trying to force yourself into something that will fuck your life up." Block was honest with him because he knew Sean had a bright future.

"Block, I made my mind up."

"I'ight, let me go holla at daddy real quick." Block went upstairs after taking his food out of the microwave.

Sosa waited in the kitchen, hoping his dad wouldn't wild out on him. But Sosa already had in mind what he would do if his dad told him no. He had plans to rob local drug dealers until the gang was on their feet.

Twenty minutes later, Block came back downstairs with a strange look on his face.

"To my surprise, he wants to talk with you."

"What he say?" Sosa asked.

"I told him that you wanna sell drugs, and you wasn't taking no for an answer," Block said.

"Nice way to word it, fucking clown." Sosa went upstairs, hearing Block laugh.

Barry's room was upstairs, next to his sister's room at the end of the hallway.

Sosa knocked twice and asked to enter, showing respect. His dad was a Muslim, so asking to enter a person's room was a part of Barry's deen. Even though Sosa wasn't a Muslim, he still respected his dad's religion. Growing up in Philly, everybody was mostly Muslim, so he was used to the ways and culture.

"Come inside," Barry yelled from inside the room.

His dad's room smelled like Muslim oil and candles. It was hooked up with a mink rug, flat screen TV, bookshelves, and a fireplace built into the wall.

"What's up, pops?"

"Sit in the chair and listen because we are only gonna have this talk once." Barry's voice was stern, as he sat on the edge of the bed.

"Ok." Sosa did as he was told.

"Once you in this game, the ways out are jail or death. There is no folding or quitting when shit gets real. I been in this game since a little kid because my mom or dad ain't have none of this luxury. I had to find a way for my parents and siblings to eat and keep a roof over their heads. When Philly was rough, I climbed the ladder and became a kingpin, but not overnight. I had to kill a lot of my close friends for betrayal. This money will make your friends and family turn on you in a second. I risked my life so you, Zarhya, and Block could live a better lifestyle than I had growing up. And now I hear you want to follow in my footsteps, just like Block. Me and Block had this same conversation when he turned 18. But the big difference between you and him is you're a lot more intelligent than him. I had hoped for you and Zarhya both to go straight to college. But as a man, I understand why you want to do this. You want the big house, nice car, nice women, big jewelry, and to feed your homies. That's not what the game is about. If you gonna hustle, do it for yourself and family. I'm let you make your own choices in life, but I'll tell you this. If you cross me, snake me, or rat, I will kill you myself. It's no love in business, at all, so you better pray your heart turns cold quick. I won't be selling you shit, Block will. All your bossy affairs should be dealt with through him, period," Barry said, still disappointed he was about to put his son in the game.

"Thanks, pops. I won't let you down. I have a team to sell it, and everything is in place." Sosa was happy.

"Not so fast. You got twenty-four hours to get your shit and move out my house. Here go $10,000. You wanna be a man? Here you go." Barry handed Sosa the money.

"I understand."

"I know you do but understand the rules to the game because one slip up could end your career. Now get out my room," Barry said, as Sosa shot out to go holla at Block, his new plug.

Chapter 3

North Philly

Block took Sosa out to a bar called Playhouse, which was normally packed on weekends, but on weeknights it wasn't so much going on, so he came out with Sosa.

When Sosa came and told him his father let him into the family business, he wasn't surprised, especially hearing Barry kick him out the house.

For their father to give Sosa the green light, Block knew he had to see something in the young man that he didn't see because Block really dubbed his little brother's survival skills in the streets.

"I can't believe daddy put me out," Sosa said, sitting in a small booth as Block ordered some drinks, mainly for himself because Sosa disliked drinking.

"Don't feel bad, little bro. When I started to sell drugs, he kicked me out. At least he gave you some money, I had to use Maggie and what I had saved up." Block remembered when Barry did him the same way.

"I know he don't want this type of lifestyle surrounding Zarhya."

"Facts. She still think daddy is a business owner and shit."

"Well, he did own that butcher shop," said Sosa, who worked there for two summers a few years back.

"That's a front, my nigga. Let's be real," Block laughed, seeing his drinks arrive.

"Now we're gonna be in business. I ask you to look at me as a client, and not a brother," Sosa said.

"Shit, that's how it goes anyway, cuz. But to be a hunnid, I don't think you ready," Block voiced his real concern.

"Me being here is not based upon what you think or feel. I may be a school nigga, but I'm also street smart."

"How can you be street smart if you never played in the streets? If you have to kill a nigga, do your really think it's in your heart, bro?" Block asked.

"I'ma do whatever it takes."

"Ok, I hear you. But since you gonna be copping from me, I don't need to be uncertain that if a nigga rob you he came off with an easy lick. These niggas ain't playing out here, Sean."

"I understand where you're coming from, and I am holding my own out here. Don't doubt me or mistrust me until I give you a reason to," Sosa told him, seeing a few cute chicks enter the bar. But a woman was his last worry.

"Who do you plan on selling the keys to, high school kids?" Block joked.

"Nah, bro, I got some people I know waiting on me."

"Can you trust them niggas? Shit be all good when the money start flowing, but when the feds start watching, niggas start dropping."

"My people solid," Sosa stated, not trying to give too much info about his boys.

"I need you to take a ride with me real quick," Block said, taking his last shot of Henny, gulping it down.

Sosa followed his brother out of the bar, wondering where they were going. Knowing Block, he probably wanted to ride around and talk shit about how much money he got and how the streets work.

Block arrived in a section called Badlands, where the Dominicans and Puerto Ricans ran with an iron, selling weight. Block parked across the street from a tall building. People were going in and out, some copping drugs, and others lived there.

"What are we doing here?" Sosa asked, seeing Block zoom into the building as if he was waiting for someone to come out.

"There is a Puerto Rican man, who should be coming out that building over there any second. His name is Evil," Block said.

"Oh, you about to go speak to him?"

"No. You're about to kill him." Block pulled out a long handgun and tried to pass it to Sosa, who looked at him.

"What do you think I am, your hitman?" Sosa shot back.

"You look really shaky, and I need to know if I can trust you," Block said, seeing Evil walk out of his building in an all-white outfit with a big Cuban chain on his neck.

"That's him?" Sosa asked, seeing Evil about to cross the street.

"Yeah, bro, it's now or never," Block said, as Sosa hopped out the car without any further conversation, leaving Block's gun because he had his own on him.

Sosa creeped behind Evil as the biggest plug in North Philly was about to climb in his Benz truck. He was headed to go see one of his side chicks across town for a quickie, before heading out of town.

"Big Dawg," Sosa said, as Evil turned around to see who was behind him.

Boc. Boc. Boc. Boc. Boc.

Evil collapsed onto the truck with his chest busted up, looking Sosa in his eyes, before he hit the floor slowly.

Sosa snatched the chain off Evil's neck, and two of Evil's workers ran out of the building to see what was going on.

Boc. Boc. Boc. Boc.

Shots entered the building, hitting one of Evil's men, as Sosa then walked off and hopped in Block's car. Not trying to wait around, Block hit a U-turn in the street and got the fuck out of papi land.

The car was a bluffer, but now he saw the kid was a natural killer.

"You ok?" Block asked.

"Couldn't be better. Now, when I get my first package?"

"Tomorrow night."

"I'ight bet," Sosa said, now tucking his weapon.

"How did you get a gun?" Block asked.

Sosa laughed and turned up the car radio, seeing a few signs saying apartments for lease downtown. He memorized the number so tomorrow he could move out of his father's house.

Killing Evil didn't faze him one bit because Sosa knew murdering would be a part of his daily lifestyle soon, especially going at it with the Outlaws, who were known for their murder game.

***

25

Sosa had told Lil Hak, Twin, and Lez to bring everybody who would be the main key players for the gang so they could all have a sit down because it was time.

Lil Hak's cousin let them use her crib for a few hours while she went out to a friend's house for the evening.

"They cleared out the living room so everybody could fit inside the project apartment. Sosa knew everybody in the room. A couple of dudes may have seen him around here and there, but never knew or gave a fuck who the quiet kid was.

"Thanks for pulling up everybody. I know who all seven of you are, and for the three who don't really know me, today you will. I'm Sosa from Southwest Philly, and we about to take this shit to another level, cuz," said Sosa, as Zels and Lil Bean looked at each other. People always heard there was a nigga named Sosa, but some thought he was dead, a ghost, or locked up, doing a life bid

"I know you," Big Lack, who was Lez's best friend, said.

"Yes, I know you, too, Big Lack," Sosa replied. The last time he saw the big giant, he was choking out a nigga in front of a corner store over five hundred dollars.

"So you're the famous Sosa?" Trilla said. He was Lil Hak's shooter, with a few bodies under his belt.

"Today will be the start of a new legacy because the Sosa Gang ran up a bag and we all ate," Sosa said, passing everybody a book bag.

"What's this?" Zels peeped into the bag, seeing it was a little heavy.

When Zels saw the white bricks, he dropped the book bag like it was on fire and burned his hand, making Lez laugh.

"There are six keys in each bag. Three keys are for each of you, and the other three is the profit you bring me so we can re-up and elevate to a bigger level," Sosa said, seeing the whole gang smiling, ready to flood their hoods.

"Damn, bull, niggas about to be on," Lez said.

Twin gave Sosa a hug because his boy did it, and not for himself, but for the guys.

"I wanna add, a key go for forty-two right now, so we should be able to make a killing. I've been hearing niggas shit is stepped on right now," Lil Hak added.

"Be on point with the Outlaws because, once word get out we getting money, the trouble will come ten times faster," Lez said.

"Swank's death got them niggas going crazy right now, all over the city," Zels said with a laugh.

"Fuck them. It's time to focus on us. Let's run it up," Sosa said, ending the get-together.

Romell Tukes

Chapter 4

North Philly
Present Day

Sosa drove his Maserati truck to Temple University College to meet up with Zarhya to take her out for a lunch date. He had been so busy lately that brother and sister time seemed rare.

Riding through the city, listening to PNB Rock, made him flashback to twenty-four months ago, when he jumped in the coke game. Looking back to the moment he told his father that this was the life he wanted, brought a smile to his face. Now he was that nigga.

In two years, Sosa Gang went from a bunch of young niggas, running around Philly, dirty and hungry, looking for a chance at any type of money just to survive.

Today, every nigga in the gang was eating off a big plate all over Philly. The crew had been locking shit down, thanks to Sosa setting it out. Sosa started out with forty-two keys that his brother Block gave him, and now he is playing with a few hundred daily.

Every week, Sosa was meeting Block to re-up so he could see his crew eat, which was all he ever wanted. Life felt like it was coming together for him. At twenty years old, there was nothing he didn't desired and couldn't get. He levied the motto money could buy the world.

Seeing there was still a half of hour left before Zarhya got out of school for her break, he stopped at a Starbucks coffee shop on the college campus.

Pulling into the large college, he wondered what it would have been like to attend college as he'd planned to growing up, until he saw how his brother and dad were living a boss lifestyle off drugs.

Being in the game, Sosa learned how to carefully premeditate each step of his plans so she didn't slip, or become a victim to a jail cell, like a lot of his niggas.

Summer was a few months ago, and Sosa knew it would be a lit summer because the gang had their money up. Beef with the Outlaws had been like a rollercoaster, as bodies dropped and niggas got locked up on all type of charges, murders, shootings, drugs, and, of course, the R.I.C.O. on federal indictments.

Luckily, Sosa and the top leaders managed to stay under the radar, while everybody else turned the city to a battlefield.

The head leader of the D.C. crew, Wayne, was locked up on two bodies, while his little brother, Roddy, held them down.

Crispy and Sin were still running the Outlaws, waging war on any nigga claiming Sosa Gang, and it was vice versa.

Sosa had just recently started drinking coffee, about two months ago, and he'd become addicted. Since he didn't use drugs, and rarely drank, coffee was now his go-to addiction.

Sosa walked into Starbucks and ordered a nice, hot coffee. Then he went outside, grabbing today's Philadelphia Inquirer newspaper to read, as if he was an old man. But Sosa found peace in reading while drinking coffee.

Out of the corner of his eye, he saw one of the most beautiful women he'd ever laid eyes on. Trying not to stare became a challenge. She was so stunning that he felt his heart rate speed up a notch.

Trying to think of something to say, he had a brain fart, which wasn't like him. Talking to women was his lane.

He saw she was on her laptop, typing something, maybe for school.

"Excuse me, but is there Wi-Fi here?" Sosa asked her.

"I believe so." The woman looked up, gave him a friendly smile, and put her head back into her laptop, working on a school essay.

Sosa cursed himself for asking some dumb shit. He tried to think of something else, but couldn't even clearly focus at the moment.

Looking over her shoulder, she finally caught him, and gave him a blank look, trying to figure out what he was looking at.

Ten minutes later, the sexy, dark skin woman stood up. Sosa saw her thin waist and curves poking out, knowing her ass had to be phat.

The lady packed up her bag and walked off, but Sosa saw she'd left her phone and wallet with Louis Vuitton logos on it.

He jumped up so fast that the coffee almost spilled over. But Sosa didn't give a fuck, he wasn't about to miss his big opportunity. Sosa picked up her items and saw the eye candy walking to the parking lot next to the administration building.

"Pardon me," he yelled.

She stopped, hoping Sosa wasn't a stalker because she'd seen the weird stares.

"Yes?"

"This is yours. I saw you left it." Sosa handed her the phone and wallet.

"Oh my God, thank you. I can't believe I left that back there," she said.

"No problem." Sosa froze, not knowing where to go from here. All he could do was put his head down.

"I'm Karlee." She extended her hand, sensing he was nervous.

"I'm Sosa."

"That's your pre-name? Your given name?" She shot back with a smile, showing all thirty-two teeth.

Karlee had chinky eyes, dark skin, long, jet black hair, and a toned body with a phat ass. She was in her last year of med school at Temple University.

"Oh, sorry, my real name is Sean. My family calls me that."

"Well then, you go to school here? I never saw you," she said.

"No, I don't. My sister, Zarhya, goes here. It's her freshman year, and I came to take her out to lunch."

"That's sweet. Well, I don't want to hold you up, Sean. Thank you for returning this. Most people would have left it or taken it. I saw a white guy steal this girl's purse, two weeks ago. And when I said something to him, he told me to fuck off," Karlee said, shaking her head.

"Damn, people are shiesty."

"Odee…"

"I would like to see you again if possible, Karlee?"

"Uhmmm, I don't know, Sean. You look like a playboy," she joked, but really thought he was very handsome.

"Not at all. I wouldn't even waste your time, if that was my characteristics."

"I definitely feel that. Well take my number and call me whenever. But I be odee bossy with school. This is my last year, so it's crunch time for me," she said.

"What's your major?"

"Med school. They have a section on the other side of the school for med students."

"That's cool. Let me grab my phone real quick." Sosa ran to his Maserati, which was parked a few cars down.

When she saw it, the thought of asking him how he go that expensive truck crossed her mind, but she didn't want to seem tumultuous.

"Nice car." she couldn't help giving him an arched eyebrow, which he didn't catch.

"Thanks," Sosa replied, as they exchanged numbers and went their way.

Sosa called Zarhya to see where she was at. To his surprise, she walked out of one of the buildings next to him.

Zarhya jumped in his arms when she saw him because they hadn't been around each other in three months.

"Why you ain't been coming to see me, goofy?" She punched him.

"You should've called me, big head."

"Shut up. Come on, let's go get a Philly Cheese Steak. I'm starving," she said, walking to her BMW Sedan her dad got her.

Zarhya was a pretty, brown skin, slim chick with a bossy attitude that scared dudes away because she had a line of dudes on her body.

"How's school? What's poppin' with them grades?" Sosa asked, getting into his sister's car, leaving the Maserati, hoping he wouldn't get a ticket for parking in a student parking lot.

"It's cool, easy, straight A's, but these bitches be fucking the professors in here because they dumb," she informed Sosa, telling him about the college secrets.

Romell Tukes

Chapter 5

South Philly

Saigon Projects was the heart of South Philly, besides Wilson Projects nearby. The Outlaws ran Saigon PJ's, while Sosa Gang controlled Wilson PJ's.

Crispy parked the new Audi RS 7 in front of the hood he grew up in and loved with all his heart. South Philly was his kingdom, and now he felt like it was switching on him because all the little niggas were crossing sides to Sosa Gang. That really bothered him.

It was a nice day in Philly so Crispy wore a Balenciaga outfit with his bust down AP watch, which he loved.

There were a few heads out, but his little soldier wasn't outside.

"Dell, where Dey at?" Crispy asked a worker, who was standing in the hood, selling drugs hand to hand with a dirty dope fiend.

"What's up? He in the back, on the court," Dell said, happy to see a hood legend.

"I'ight though, and word of advice, sell in the building or behind it. You know this shit hot out here, bro," Crispy told him.

"It won't happen again," Dell said, seeing two more fiends approach the block, looking for the good dog food the Outlaws had.

Crispy walked to the back, waving and nodding his head at a few people he grew up with in the hood.

Since losing his little brother, Swank, two years ago, he had a hard-on for Sosa Gang members. Crispy, and most of the city, knew the top dogs for Sosa were Lez, Lil Hak, and his number one rival, Twin, from a few blocks down.

Crispy got word that someone saw Twin leaving his brother's crime scene, and there was no doubt Twin smoked Swank. The beef between the two crews had been going for years, since he was a youngin.

For the past two years, Sosa Gang had been having a lock on the city's drug trade. Crispy found that very confusing because Sosa Gang was never about getting money.

35

Crispy felt like he was missing something, as if his ops had some type of mastermind, or shot caller, behind the scene. But when he mentioned that to Sin, he highly disagreed.

Sin addressed the issue in their last meeting, saying maybe Lez, who was smarter than them all, found a plug somewhere, and Crispy left the thought at that.

The Outlaws were run like an underworld society because they had ranks. Sin and Crispy were the faces of their group, but there were other remembers, who had a lot of power, but didn't show their faces, due to many reasons.

"Dawg," Crispy yelled, walking on the basketball court to see over twenty bottles on the ground and blunt wraps all over the place.

"Crispy, where you been, scrap," Dawgg said, glad to see his young, old head.

Crispy put Dawgg onto a bag years ago, around West Philly, shooting up shit for no reason.

When Crispy snatched him up, he was getting grain man money. Dawgg's sister was a chick from West Philly. She had a bag also.

"Niggas is out here today."

"Yeah, we having the candlelight for Tum G today," Dawgg said sadly

"I heard about that, bull. What happened?"

"He got caught slippin' last night, shooting dice, when Zels and the niggas spinned through the parking lot. First they missed, and then Zels spinned the block again and killed Tum G, hitting Grid twice. But he pulled through," Dawg said.

"Fuck."

"Niggas in their bag out here," Dawgg said, as a couple of dudes brought out their dirt bikes and raced through the projects.

"Y'all strapped?"

"Everybody got heat, cuz," Dawgg lifted his shirt, showing a 226 Sig 9mm 15 shot handgun on his hip.

"The money is still moving, bull? I know it's hot out here, so only have two or three niggas out, and one on watch, just in case the police spin through." Crispy looked around to see more than forty niggas out, ready to air something.

"That's already in motion, bro."

"This weekend the new product supposed to arrive, so be ready when I call."

"I was born ready," Dawgg replied, seeing two groups of chicks join the party, coming in from the back side to get high and drunk with the guys.

"Max about to touch in a few days, so he's gonna have Southwest in a headlock, and North Philly," Crispy said, thinking about his young shooter, who was supposed to be released from prison soon.

"That's my bro, but them D.C. crew niggas be heavy over the north, and you know how they feel about us," Dawgg stated.

"Fuck them niggas. They nothing without Wayne," Crispy said.

"Roddy ain't shit to sleep on, cuz. I saw him in action." Dawgg knew Roddy personally. He was laid back, but cold-blooded, just like his brother Wayne.

"Max will handle that when he touches down. We got people over there, so they will be fine. But I gotta go. Be safe out here, bull." Crispy embraced Dawgg and dapped up a couple of his youngins before leaving.

***

Northeast Philly

King Blood walked into a trap house in a hood called Oxford Circle, a new high drug traffic area.

Knock. Knock.

A tall, skinny, yellow nigga with big teeth answered the door, seeing King Blood had a book bag on his back, which he assumed was the money for the work.

"Come in, right on time," Diesel said, moving out the doorway so his new client could enter. Diesel sold weight for Block. He was from Chester, a city outside of Philly that was known for money and violence also, but not as crazy as the city of Brotherly Love.

"My people told me a lot about you," King Blood stated, walking into the trap, looking around to see if anybody else was in there. He hated doing business in the presence of other people.

"Niggas told me you spend heavy so it's all love. I got the seventeen keys here in the kitchen for you. I'ma throw you three joints on the arm. Get me back when you can, bro," Diesel said, walking him into the kitchen.

"That's real. I'ma be back to see you real soon, if it's fire," King Blood replied, taking off his backpack and handing it to Diesel, while looking at the twenty keys on the table.

Diesel looked into the bag to count the money and saw nothing but some gym clothes inside, and two garbage bags.

When Diesel lifted his head up, King Blood had his gun already aimed at Diesel's face.

"Say it wit me, bro. I was looking," King Blood said smiling.

"You got me, dog. To take to my life ain't worth it, bro," Diesel said, trying to play it cool. But he was really terrified out of his mind.

"I would let you slide, but I can't for two reasons," King Blood told him, before looking at the time of his watch because he had somewhere to be real soon.

"Come on, bro. I won't tell nobody. I swear on my soul, cuz."

"I can't take the risk for you to blow my cover. That's one reason. And number two, I'm a cop," King Blood said.

"What? The pigs?"

"More like dirty pig, you feel me?" King Blood laughed.

"I got lawyer money. Plus, this shit cut so much by the time it comes back from the lab that twenty keys may come back to 50 grams," Diesel laughed, happy that King Blood was a cop and not a robber.

"I don't think you get it. I'm a dirty cop. Better for when I clock in at the 25th police station," King Blood, whose real name was Officer Kilow, said before placing the keys in a garbage bag and leaving the crime scene to start his day at the precinct.

Chapter 6

West Philly

"Nigga, I bet two bands on the 76ers tonight," Lil Bean said.

"Two? Nigga, I got five bands with the Raptors. What you trying to do, scrap?" Lez said, coming into the living room.

The gang was watching the opening season of the NBA at Big Lack's apartment on 49th Street and Lancaster.

"Five is a bet, old head," Lil Bean said, counting out five thousand from a wad of money he had on him and placing it on the table.

"You trying to get in, Big Lack?" Lez asked his boy, who was making a cup of lean.

"I'm Muslim, bull. I don't gamble," Big Lack said seriously, making Lil Bean and Lez both laugh hard.

"We all Muslim, bull, but that shit don't stop your big ass from pouring a 8th of lean and killing niggas out here," Lez replied.

"And you sell drugs, nigga," Bean added, getting ready for the game.

"Allah said no man will be perfect in this world," Big Lack said.

"Nigga, you know what the fuck you be doing," Lil Bean shouted.

"Y'all heard about Tum C and them niggas?" Big Lack changed the subject because he took his religion serious and hated when people played with it

"Hell yeah. I hated that nigga," Lil Bean said.

"Zels and his boys spinned the bin on them clown ass niggas," Lez said.

"Dawgg sick, I bet," Big Lack added, taking a sip of the purple lean and loving the taste he'd been addicted to for years now.

"Ayo, ain't Dawgg your ex-girlfriend step-brother or some shit?" Lil Bean asked, already knowing the answer. He just loved getting under people's skin, especially Lez because it was easy.

"Bean, you know that's Foxy's brother. Stop asking dumb shit," Lez said, rolling a blunt of sour, smoking on a Tum C pack, which was smoking on a dead op.

"Whatever happened to Foxy and you, cuz? Shawty was official, bro. She used to be around the gang all day, and she had some bad bitches with her," Big Lack said, remembering when he tried to bag three of Foxy's home girls, but they curved him.

"Facts," Lil Bean added.

"Shit ain't work out, bro. We grew apart, cuz. I had been with her since a little kid," Lez said.

"Nigga, that mean you got caught cheating," Big Lack replied, joking on Lez for losing a bad bitch like Foxy.

"Can we just watch the game, ock? I ain't come over here for joke time, Scrap." Lez got upset.

"When Sosa pulling up with some more work?" Lil Bean asked. He was down to four keys, and he knew two niggas who wanted it ASAP.

"I don't know, bro, but I'm on to right now." Lez figured he would give Sosa a call tomorrow to see what was up with the next load.

"This shit crazy, bro. Two years ago, I was living at my mom's crib, asking her for money. Now I got my own spot with a big body Benz truck out front, and mama love got one too," Big Lack said, thankful to be a part of the strong movement running the city.

"Sosa made a way for us all," Lez said, as everybody nodded their heads in agreement.

"We really lit right now, bro. The only thing that's slowing us down is the ops," Lil Bean said.

"Facts. Beef make the city hot." Big Lack hated warring, but they had no choice.

"It's either them or us, cuz. And niggas know who Sin and Crispy coming for, so we gotta go hard and hold shit down," Lez said, as the game came on TV and they focused on the opening games.

"I got five bands on the 76ers," Big Lack said.

"Nigga, hell no. You was just popping wild shit," Lez said.

"You too late, bro. The game started," Lil Bean added.

"Fuck y'all." Big Lack went to take a shit.

Sosa Gang

***

Downtown Philly

Foxy and two of her home-girls were shopping at the Gallery Mall, doing what they did best.

"Let's go up in here. I heard they got some new Louis Vuitton purses that just came out," Foxy's friend CeeCee said, who was a dancer and scammer.

All of Foxy girls were hustlers, some danced at strip clubs, some sold drugs, a lot of them scammed, and some even made legit money off social media, like Foxy.

"Bitch, don't get caught like you did in the Chanel store at Franklin Mills Mall," Ashley said, already knowing CeeCee was about to swap some shit because that was her side hustle.

"Girl, you always bringing up old shit," CeeCee shot back.

"Bitch, that was just last week I had to bail you out," Foxy said, walking into the Louis Vuitton store.

"You're always on her side." CeeCee made them laugh.

Foxy loved her girls. She had so many home-girls that she made days to chill with each group of them. Foxy was very appealing, with smooth dark skin, thick sexy curves, tatts on her thighs and legs, bright brown eyes, long slick hair, and a nice smile. She was Jamaican and Black, and one of the baddest chicks on the west side of Philly.

She made a lot of money off her social media because Foxy was considered an Instagram Model, with 7.5 million followers. Her second hustle was scamming, whenever she felt like it, unlike her girls, who had to. Foxy's dad wasn't in the picture. He'd been gone since she was a kid, and Foxy didn't care. She loved her hardworking mother and her brother, Dawgg, who shared the same mom but different fathers.

"Foxy, I saw Lez and his crew in the club last week. Them nigga was squad deep. I swear they had to drop over 100,000 in that bitch," CeeCee said, picking out items she planned to swap.

"I don't care. Why are you telling me this?" Foxy caught an attitude.

"Damn, I'm just saying, he looks good and is getting some real money," CeeCee said.

"Unlike you and Ashely, I don't sack chase. I don't need no nigga for nothing except some good dick, maybe," Foxy said.

"What I got to do with that?" Ashley said.

"Ashley, we all know you be sucking them old niggas' dicks," CeeCee said, making Foxy and another woman, who was shopping and eavesdropping, laugh.

"So. As long as he paying, I'll suck a monkey's dick," Ashely replied, making her girls crack up laughing.

"Lez was a cheater. I gave him chance after chance, and he kept fucking up. So I couldn't kept getting myself in those phases because I'm loyal to my man, especially if he treats me right," Foxy said.

"So, you never cheated?" Ashely asked.

"No, but when I found out he was doing him, I was texting niggas to get it out of my head. But I couldn't cheat. I was bigger than that." Foxy remembered the nights she wanted to fuck other niggas just to get back.

"If that nigga had to do a bid, would you have been there for him?" CeeCee asked because she was holding her man down on a five year bid.

"Hell yeah. If he was a real nigga to me, I'd be there because I would have to put myself in his shoes. Doing jail time be hard and everybody need support. Then bitches be looking stupid when they man come home and do them wrong because they left them for dead," Foxy said, as Ashely and CeeCee both brought their shit to the register to check out.

"What about them goofy dudes that come home after a bitch did a bid with them and shit on her?" CeeCee said.

"You got a lot of those niggas. That's why you have to know your man in and out. It's not hard," Foxy said, schooling them.

"It's like taking a risk," Ashley said, seeing the cards they stole work.

"Life is about risks, but I'll tell you, I'm not doing no double digits unless he my husband. Anything over eight, I'm done," Foxy said.

"Shit, eight is too long. Anything over eight months, I'm out," Ashley said.

"That's why you ain't got no man, bitch," CeeCee said.

"And I don't want one. I'm in love with the money," Ashely said.

"I bet." Foxy walked out the store, wanting to go to the Tiffany & Co. jewelry store to buy her mama a bracelet for her birthday in two weeks.

***

South West Philly

Twin went to Imam Ahmad's Mosque to make his afternoon prayer real quick, before he met up with P. Cok to drop him off the rest of some work he got.

Running the streets day and night, sometimes he forgot to pray. Being born a Muslim and raised in an Islamic household, some things stuck with him, but making his five daily prayers wasn't one.

"How have you been?" Imam Ahmad came out back, when he saw Twin finish up praying on camera.

"As-salaam-alaikum, pops."

"Wa-alaikum-salaam," Imam Ahmad replied, sitting next to his son, one of three kids.

"I been good maintenance."

"I saw you last week with your friends, downtown. You are judged by the friends you have, and the wise never get aligned with fools. Wise friends chase away sorrows, and the foolish ones gather them." Imam Ahmad always had a way with his words. He was a wise man that had been through a lot in his day. He was one of the city's most respected Imam's.

"That's real, pops. I stay awake, old head."

"I hope so, because sometimes we may think we are wide awake, but in reality we are sleep." Imam Ahmad got up in his Islamic garment, hugging his youngest son before going off to the back, where he came from.

Chapter 7

Green County State Prison, PA

Gee posted up in the prison yard with a handful of Sosa Gang niggas he'd known for a long time, since running around in the streets as a wild youngin.

When he got sentenced to a bid for a violent charge, Gee was sick, until he realized all he had to do off of five years was three and a half years. With a year left, Gee now had his focus on going home and getting to his family, and the love of his life, Latifah.

Since being locked up in prison, Latifah and Gee's sister, Shierka, had been holding him down to the fullest on every visit, money, and letter.

All of his boys were there a hunnid for him, also, with whatever he needed, and that was a big blessing.

Being from 23th and Hunting in North Philly, the street lifestyle was exposed to him at a young age. So when hopping off the porch, he jumped right in the field.

The block he was from were majority Sosa Gang members and the D.C. crew, but now, since he had been gone, word was Sosa Gang took over. Every new nigga that arrived from Philly told Gee how his bulls were out there getting real money and laying shit down.

Gee wasn't surprised about the beef with the Outlaws because shit was lit when he was home. But to hear the gang making big money moves flipping bricks, surprised him.

Gee wanted to find a job and leave the streets alone, because coming back to jail wasn't in the plans anymore.

There were close to sixty Sosa Gang niggas in the jail, but also a lot of Outlaw niggas running around. Gee was the leader of his gang in the prison, and a kid named Max ran the Outlaws in there. The beef between Sosa Gang and Outlaws didn't hold too much weight in state prison because mostly everybody was Muslim and had a truce until released. But niggas were still cliqued up.

In PA state prisons the main beef was normally between Philly and Pittsburg niggas, who secretly hated each other.

Gee watched the chess game in the yard with his boys, waiting to go back on rec call so he could use the phone.

"I heard the bull, Omelly, came thru North Philly in a Wraith this weekend, and dropped forty bands in a dice game in Uptown," Problem said, who was a Sosa Gang nigga from North Philly in Thompson Projects.

"That's the bro," Tatted Mike replied.

"Nigga, you don't even know that nigga. You been locked up twelve years, since you was sixteen," Gee said, knowing Tatted Mike be capping.

"Nah, I heard of him, bro." Tatted Mike was the oldest Sosa Gang bull in the prison, with a double life sentence for killing two D.C. crew niggas at a high school, when he was a youngin.

"Let Mike think whatever he wants. Y'all know he burnt out," Moon B said, playing chess, making them all laugh as a group of Outlaw niggas walked by mean mugging them, as they always did

"I really hate them niggas, bull," Problem said.

"Fuck them. They not a threat, cuz," Gee replied, knowing Problem disliked the ops, who shot him twice and killed his older cousin.

"Nigga said Diesel got killed the other night. Bull was a live wire, too," Tru said, approaching them after playing a giver on five basketball game, with Philly versus Pittsburg, something they did in the jail every weekend to keep the peace.

"Damn, I know Dawgg and them dudes from Saigon Projects sick, cuz," Problem said.

"When they find out who did it, I know Dawgg gonna act up," Tatted Mike said, next up to play a game of chess.

"Shit, they already know it was Lil Zels," Tru said.

"That's my little bro. Niggas ain't fucking with him. The bull a straight hitter though," Problem told them.

"They say the bull spinned the block twice on Diesel because he missed the first time," Tru said, shaking his head, glad he was in jail.

Sosa Gang

"It's going to be a cold summer out here," Gee said, not trying to go back home to the dumb shit and get jammed up.

***

South Philly

Dawgg hid behind the tins of the Dodge minivan, with four shooters sitting behind him, waiting on the greenlight. They were parked on 5th and Moore, a Sosa Gang turf. Twin ran with Zels and a crew of little niggas, causing havoc.

"Mooky, you sure this fool live here?" Dawgg asked his little cousin, who was cool with Frank, a known shooter for Twin, and a money getting nigga.

"Look. That's him walking up the block on his phone, Ski," yelled Mooky.

Dawgg started up the rental van, keeping the lights off, as he creeped down the block on a late night. Luckily, nobody was out.

Frank was so caught up in texting his girl to let her know he was on the block about to come upstairs, he ain't notice four shooters hop out, until it was too late.

The Outlaws jumped Frank, who was only five-five and weighing nothing, making it easy for them to toss him in the van like a toy.

Dawgg drove a few blocks down to 7th and McKean, where a line of abandoned row houses were.

"Throw that nigga over there," Dawgg told his crew, once inside the open back door, which fiends used to come in and out. They would use the abandoned buildings as a trap house to get high.

"Dawgg and Mooky, it ain't gotta be like this. I swear, I ain't have shit to do with Diesel's death. That's the bro," Frank said lying. The night Zels killed Diesel, he was the driver.

"Shut the fuck up," Mooky yelled as his voice echoed in the empty, stanky house.

"You love your gang, Frank?" Dawgg asked, pulling out some thick rope and a gun from a backpack one of his soldiers handed him.

"Hell nah. I love South Philly. We all family out here," Frank said, trying to figure out what Dawgg was about to do with the rope and gun. Frank had a gift of gab. He could talk himself out the hell fire.

Dawgg saw his mom calling, but it was really bad timing so he ignored it, knowing she just wanted to check up on him.

"Where are Zels and Twin hiding out? For some reason, I can't find them anywhere," Dawgg asked, walking to Frank, who was in the corner of the room.

"I don't fuck with neither one of them niggas, real rap," Frank said.

"He's lying," Mooky said, knowing Frank too well.

"Mooky, I would never lie to you. We used to be best friends, bro. We fucked bitches together and all of that," Frank said.

"Nigga, she was your cousin," Mooky replied, remembering the time Frank set him up with a thot and they got her drunk and both fucked the chick, to only find out the girl was Frank's first cousin.

"Same shit," Frank said.

Dawgg laughed at how low-down Frank had to be, but he knew South Philly niggas were the grimiest of them all.

"One last time, Lil Frank, where can I find Zels and Twin, or at least one of them?" Dawgg asked, now with his gun aimed at Frank's face.

"Ok. Ok. Ok," Frank pleaded.

"I told you it would be too easy," Mooky said, smiling because it was his idea to snatch Frank up at his girl's house.

"Y'all listen," Frank said, taking a deep breath, knowing he was about to regret what he was about to tell them, but deep down, it was the right thing to do.

"Talk, hurry up." Dawgg got upset, inching closer to his face.

"Suck my big dick," Frank yelled before spitting a hock of spit in Dawgg's face.

Boc. Boc. Boc. Boc. Boc. Boc. Boc. Boc.

Dawgg stopped firing and wiped the spit from his face, pissed off.

"Hang this nigga on the 5th and Moore light pole with this rope. I don't give a fuck how you do it, just get it done now," Dawgg yelled, leaving his boys with the rope and weapon.

Romell Tukes

Chapter 8

Darby, PA

On the outskirts of Philly lay a nice middle and upper class area called Darby, where Sin recently moved, just to get out of the hood and into a new environment. The mini mansion was built for a king, with a lushly landscape that blended in with the neighborhood, a two-story entrance, premium hardwood floors, government kitchen, architectural designed ceiling to floor windows, club room, movie theater, six bedrooms, five bathrooms, and a four-car garage for his luxury cars.

At twenty-seven years old, Sin felt like his life wouldn't be any better than this, but there was one thing he was at odds with, the Sosa Gang.

Sin just wanted to make some money and live life worrying with half the city but he was too deep in the beef to complain now especially after losing a bunch of men.

For the last two years Sosa Gang been slowing his paper down because words was they had some good product. Sin only knew of a few niggas in Philly who were moving weight and he was one, so whoever supplied them had to be from out of town, he gathered.

Sin couldn't see Lez, Lil Hak, nor Twin finding a sturdy plug. He was starting to think maybe Crispy was on point about how someone else could be calling the shots. If that was the case, then he could find out who and end their little run. Without money and power, nobody will respect you. Being one of the top members in the Outlaws consisted of many roles, but Sin's main goal was to make sure his people ate.

Tonight, he had to meet up with his plug-in a nearby city, so they could go over the details of his next pick up.

Sin looked at the money machine and all the stacks of money surrounding the table. He felt like Scarface, before he got killed.

Crispy texted him earlier, telling Sin he would be by soon with some chicks. But Sin had one of his baby mamas upstairs. He planned to kick her out when he got done counting the re-up money.

Sin loved his kids, mom, sister, and even his gay brother, who he'd just started talking to, ten years after finding out he was gay. Sin knew family was important, so he looked past his brother being gay, and treated him like family.

He heard his baby's mother upstairs calling him. Already knowing she wanted a quickie, Sin paused what he was doing to get his nut.

***

Southwest, Philly

Lil Hak and Zels watched the big basketball tournament going on in the park next to Bartram Village. This was Lil Hak's hood. Larchwood and Greenway were also his stomping grounds in Southwest.

Zels came out to get away from South Philly for a couple of days, after what happened that morning.

When the Sosa Gang niggas came outside that morning, they saw Frank hanging ass naked from a rope on a street light, with his penis cut off.

The second Zels heard the disturbing news, he gathered up a car load of shooters, and sent another car of gunmen to Saigon PJs, while he went to Tasker Projects to shoot the shit up. And both crews did just that.

Early that morning, five people were shot, and two of them pronounced dead at the scene, thanks to the Sosa Gang.

South Philly had police and the FEDS flooding the area as an off-duty cop got shot in the crossfire.

"They left Lil Frank fucked up like that, young bull?" Lil Hak asked Zels as they were both surrounded by shooters in the park.

"Bro, that shit crazy. I know it's from that Diesel shit, you hear me," Zels said, taking sip of lean.

"Y'all did the right thing, airing out Saigon and Tasker PJs," Lil Hak said.

"Fact. We had to do something. I wasn't about to let them goofies get up on us, cuz. Big facts." Zels knew the early morning attack would send a big message.

"They killed one of us, we hit two of their bro's," Lil Hak added.

"Facts. I ain't even speak to Twin yet, but he in Da Bottom anyway."

"That nigga's always down there. Ain't shit on 39th and Mount Vernon."

"Shit, that's where all the money at, bull. Twin is making that paper down there, and in Wilson PJ's," Zels said.

"No worries. Why the bull don't want nobody down there with him?" Lil Hak asked.

"Facts. But Sosa is about to get it right this week, right?" Zels asked.

"I believe so, but now, since that shit going on around your way, I think it will be smart to just breathe easy for a few weeks, especially with the FEDS in town. Sosa ain't trying to fuck with them boys," Lil Hak said, seeing his team lose.

"That makes sense," Zels said, seeing Twin finally call his phone. Most likely it was to talk about what happened that morning, but Zels knew he made the right call.

***

Downtown Philly

Club Aces on a Monday was still jumping, and Block came out, not only to chill with his girl Maggie, who was a bottle girl and bartender.

"I haven't saw you come to my job in a long time. Don't you get enough of this brown sugar at home?" Maggie said, sitting in his lap.

"I'll never get enough of this good coochie, baby girl. You know that," Block said, rubbing on her phat pussy through the booty shorts she worked in to attract males to buy drinks and bottles in the club.

"So, who was that Erica B I saw in your phone last night when you was sleep, nigga?" She asked over the loud music, taking him by surprise.

"Who me?"

"Yeah, you, nigga. Don't play dumb," she spit back, seeing Sosa walk into the booth section.

"Sean," Block yelled happily. His little brother saved the day. Plus, he was waiting on him anyway.

"We will finish this later," Maggie said, getting up to leave. She left him to Sosa, who she knew as Sean.

Sosa couldn't help but to take a quick glimpse at her ass.

"What's good, bull?" Sosa said, sitting down.

"You saved the day. She was just starting to trip on a nigga," Block said, taking a sip of his drink.

"I feel you, playboy. How's business?"

"Crazy. I been in New Jersey for two fucking months. Shit got wild out here, bro. I heard the police found some little nigga hanging from a street light," Block said.

"I heard about that." Sosa saw the gruesome scene on Zels' block, so there was no doubt Zels had some dealing in that.

"Shit crazy out here, bro. I know you got your people, but it's time you cut certain ties with niggas because it's about to get thick." Block told him what Barry said in their last conversation.

"That's all he said?"

"Yes, but I've been hearing about some kid named Sosa, moving weight, sending hits in the streets, so try to stay out his way and keep doing what you're doing," Block said.

"Facts. But I'ma need double on the product today."

"You gotta wait until tomorrow," said Block.

"I'ight, call me. I got a date," Sosa said, leaving as Maggie walked back into the booth to argue with Block.

Chapter 9

Downtown Philly

When they stepped into Ruth Chris restaurant, Karlee was all smiles for their first date. She'd finally given in.

Sosa led her to a table with candles and flowers, different from the rest of the tables in the restaurant.

"Somebody put some real thought into this date, I see," Karlee said as he pulled out the chair for her.

Karlee looked like eye candy in a fire red cropped, off-the-shoulder Miu Miu dress, which she'd bought for tonight's special date.

"I had to put in a little work to show my real interest," Sosa said.

"Oh, Sean, I see you." She smiled as a chef came out to prepare their meals after taking their orders.

"This place is the bomb," Karlee stated, looking around. She had always wanted to come here, but never made the time to.

"You look beautiful. I know I've told you this twice, but it doesn't go unnoticed."

"Thank you, Mr. Handsome. We do look like a vibe together," she said.

"I feel the connection."

"That's a fact. I like talking to you."

Karlee and Sosa had talked on the phone a few hours out of the day. She loved how smart and honest he was with her, which was rare nowadays. Karlee's number one dislike, and a deal breaker, was someone who lied to her.

"Now we are face to face. What do you wanna know about me?" Sosa asked as the dim lights in the restaurant set a sexy mood.

"Ok, let me see. Where do I start?" She'd been waiting for this day.

"Shoot your shot, I'm an open book."

"Before I ask you anything, I need you to promise me, no matter what, you'll be honest?" She gave him a serious look.

"I will never lie to you, whether it's good or bad. That's not me."

"What do you do for a living?" She asked a question he knew was coming sooner or later.

"I hustle."

"Illegal or legal?"

"Drugs, Karlee. And if you gonna judge me or look at me differently for the life I chose, then I guess I'll catch you in another life," he said, seeing her face screw up.

"I'm not that type of person."

"That's good to know, but I'm not proud of what I do."

"So why do it?"

"To feed the people and not see my niggas, who I love, struggling to make nothing, or ends meet. If I can help someone, then I feel like it's my calling to do so," Sosa explained.

"It takes a lot of courage to risk your life to help others."

"Facts."

"But will they do the same for you?" She caught him off guard with that question.

"Time will tell."

"You ever wonder how some harvest manages to look good all summer, but when the season changes, it looks like it was never there?" she asked out of the blue.

"Climate change, I guess."

"When faced with different events, things change and people start to have a different outlook on things. That once blossoming beautiful crop starts to lose its beauty. Then people start to look at the once alluring harvest differently. I like to compare human nature and human characteristics the same because we are connected through creation," she said as he listened.

"I feel that, Karlee. You know how to get deep, don't you?"

"At times, I can go all day, but I'm not one to bore people."

"Shit, you will never bore me. I can listen to you all day." He made her smile.

"The other day, I was watching the news. There was first a story about how a young man was found hanging on a streetlight. I got so upset that I cried because the slave masters used to hang us the same way, just on trees, ass naked. When a male used to get hung, crowds of people used to be present for many reasons, but a main one was to see his erection. Males caught hard-ons when they used to get hung," she told him.

"I didn't know that."

"Yes. It's sad that our generation is blind to the fact of what we've been through for over four hundred years," Karlee expressed.

"I believe in justice, adequation, and equitability, but it's hard when you put what's right, against the discrimination built around you."

"That's no excuse because when you believe in something inside the heart, it becomes a part of your mind, body, and soul, so you will fight for it, no matter what. Last month, I attended a protest for a young 14-year-old kid, who got gunned down by police because they assumed he was someone else, a grown man. As I'm marching, a white lady had a sign that said freedom, so I asked her why she had that sign. Guess what she told me?" Karlee asked.

"What?" Sosa found Karlee's conversations on another level, and he loved it.

"She said it's the power or condition of acting without compulsion, and the liberty to do what you feel. I told the lady this is not freedom, when every week a black man is being killed for nothing. I went on to explain that, due to your color, certain prerogatives and privileges are foreseen." Karlee made such a strong point Sosa was blown away. But deep down, he knew him and his crew were a part of the problem.

"The date was great, at least until Karlee was ready to go back home for the long day ahead of her. They talked about each other's families and childhood. Sosa even opened up about his mom, who had mental health issues, living in Atlanta. Karlee saw how it was a soft topic, so she valued it.

***

West Philly

One of Lez's sisters, Eva, recently landed a job at the Bank of America on 36th and Market. This being her second week, she was still new as a bank teller.

The place stayed busy all day, which kept her busy, but she loved it. Eva had made plans to buy a car next week because Lez had been dropping her off and picking her up every day. She loved her brother, but Eva knew what type of shit he was into in the streets.

Watching the clock, it was five minutes to six and her shift would be done soon. Eva went to the back so she could clock out.

On her way out the door, after saying bye to a few pretty cool coworkers, she texted Lez, letting him know she was ready for him to pull up.

A Kia pulled up on the curb and rolled down its window.

"Excuse me, where can I find the Philly Zoo?" a man asked.

"It's right up the block, the way you just came from. There are signs everywhere back there. You can't miss it," Eva said, getting a weird vibe from the man.

"Thank you. I feel dumb."

"It's cool. I get lost at times, too," Eva laughed it off.

"Are you Eva?" The man asked, giving her a look as if he went to school with Eva.

"Yes."

"You don't remember me?" The man said with a smile, as she leaned into the car a little closer.

"I can't recall where I know you from?" Eva looked confused.

"From hell."

Boc. Boc. Boc. Boc. Boc.

Crispy sped off in the Kia, after giving her all face shots, killing poor Eva where she stood.

Chapter 10

West Philly

Lez left his new little bitch Valeria's crib, after beating her walls down, to pick up Eva at her new job.

Lez's aunty raised him, his brother, and his two sisters because his mom and dad were doing life sentences in prison for murders and drugs. Growing up, Lez had big basketball dreams. At six-five, he was always the tallest of the pack.

Falling into street life, Lez said fuck school. He needed clothes, food, and to take care of his household. He had been a part of Sosa Gang since elementary, controlling his section on the Westside, with over sixty members.

Lez and his older brother didn't get along at all because they were like night and day in so many ways. But little did they know, the Westside was inside both of them. His brother was Kilow, one of the dirty cops in Philly, but nobody knew they were family, not even his crew, because he didn't want them to look at him in any type of way. Lez heard a lot of vicious stories about his brother, but it did not concern him, so Lez paid it no mind.

Arriving on the block where his sister worked, he saw a bunch of cop cars and ambulances swarming the block.

"What the fuck is that?" Lez asked himself, calling Eva so he could be on his merry way because it looked like a nigga killed the president, he saw so many cops.

Lez didn't see Eva at all, as he looked around, before parking the car and getting out to see what the fuck all the commotion was about.

"Officer, I have to pick up my sister from work," Les told a young black female officer.

"Some lady got killed, so it's gonna be a minute before the bank employees of Bank of America can be released. They are giving statements," the cop said.

"Ok, cool," Lez said, about to walk off, until he saw his sister's Gucci purse on the ground, lying next to someone wrapped up in a body bag.

The cop saw the way Lez looked at the murder victim out of the corner of her eyes.

"You ok, sir?" she asked.

"Who got killed, if you don't mind me asking?"

"I can't give out any details, but since your sister works there, I'll tell you." The cop looked at the name on the notepad in her hand.

"Please."

"Eva is her first name, and last is Frozen." The cop saw Lez's face and knew this had to be his sister, as tears formed his eyes.

"Can I see my sister's body?"

"We have next of kin on the scene. Make way," the cop yelled, so he could claim the body

Lez watched as a forensic anthropologist unzipped the bag to show him the gruesome holes that the bullets made. Eva looked scary and unreal. The rage Lez felt rushed to his heart. He couldn't bear to see any more. Lez got up and walked off. Police called out for him, but he continued to walk away, not in the mood to talk.

***

North Philly
Two Days Later

Officer Kilow hadn't been himself since his sister's murder the other day. He was crushed when he got the call from a pathologist, who examines dead bodies.

Eva's photo was all over social media, with rest in peace signs. Kilow knew his sister was a good girl and didn't deserve to be murdered the way she was.

He wanted answers, and since Eva was his family, he took the case. Kilow sat in the 25th police station, trying to break the case, but he had very little to go off of.

"Kilow," Officer Hawk came into Kilow's corner section with a folder and a smile, knowing he was about to make his fellow officer's day.

"What's up Hawk?"

"Cheer up. I got good news. We were able to trace the killer's car and license plate to a young man named Bryan Bettman, aka Nosey, age twenty-two, and an Outlaw member. His rap sheet is longer than both of our dicks together. He's paroled to his apartment on 17th and Wharton in South Philly." Officer Hawk handed Kilow the file.

"Hawk, I need a big solid?'

"Anything, bro, we a team." Hawk was a dirty cop, also, and the two men did a lot of foul shit together.

"I have to go old school on this, please. I just need you to back me," Kilow begged.

"Kilow, I know that was your sister, so I got you because I believe you would do it for me."

"You're damn right, I would."

"Suit up. I'll meet you outside." Hawk walked off to get ready.

"Kilow and Hawk put on their body armor and grabbed their high power military style weapons, making their way to South Philly.

"Let's make the shit quick," Hawk said, driving through the dangerous streets, seeing young dudes selling drugs, posted up on corners, and participating in dice games, and junkies shooting up dope in the open.

Kilow looked around, watching South Philly go down the drain, turning into Zombie land. Hearing the getaway car belonged to an Outlaws member, he wondered how Eva got herself mixed up with one of the most violent crews in the city.

"This is the building right here," Kilow said, as the smoke gray Crown Vic pulled over.

"You got the search warrant, the temporary one?" Hawk asked, knowing it was too late for them to get a real warrant from the judge.

"Yep."

"Don't forget, Kilow, follow the correct outline," Hawk said, knowing if Kilow missed a step, it could be their ass.

"I got us. Come on." Kilow hopped out, seeing two young drug dealers walk off the block, thinking the cops were about to bust their balls.

Kilow led the way into the building. They walked up two flights of stairs, quietly, not trying to cause any attention to themselves.

Knock. Knock. Knock.

Kilow knocked hard on the door, hearing someone turn down a loud stereo system.

"Y'all bitches early," Nosey said, opening the door, thinking it was some hoes, who were supposed to come through.

"Walk inside with your fucking hands up," Kilow to told him.

Nosey saw the swat vests and cop outfits and knew he fucked up.

"Ok," Nosey said, doing as he was told.

"Sit down on that couch. Listen clearly. Your car was used to commit a murder two days ago in front of Bank of America," Kilow said.

"That wasn't me, bro. I swear, somebody stole my car," Nosey lied.

"The car is parked out front, lying bitch. Who did it?" Kilow yelled.

"They gonna kill me if I tell you. Just take me in," Nosey cried.

"Pick up that gun right there," Kilow said, looking at Nosey's 9mm on the table.

"What?"

"Pick it up, now," Kilow yelled, as Nosey grabbed it and lifted it to the ceiling slowly.

"Now what?" Nosey said, with the gun in the air.

"Lower it," Kilow said, as Nosey lowered his arm and the gun was pointing at Kilow and Hawk.

Boc. Boc. Boc. Boc. Boc. Boc. Boc. Boc. Boc. Boc.

Nosey's body was rattled with shots by the cops, who then called it in, saying Nosey tried to kill them, so they had to defend themselves.

Chapter 11

Downtown Philly

Sosa and the gang all met up at the Hampton Inn Hotel connected to the airport, downtown. Sosa thought it would be smart to get a room for the crew meeting today.

Everybody arrived, one by one, to not cause attention, as Sosa requested, due to the large amount of drugs inside the hotel room.

"I see everybody here, Trilla, Lil Hak, Lez, Zels, Lil Bean, Twin, and Big Lack. The gang in here. Free Gee," Sosa said, as all of them were dressed in all white, looking like real bosses.

"I'm glad we alive and all here, bull, because shit been getting crazy in dese streets," Zels started, sitting in a chair, about to pop a seal to pour himself some lean with Sprite

"Whoever had the perception that this shit would be easy, or a walk in the park on a nice sunny day, was wrong. We have more wins, but our losses will help us all become perfectionist at what we do," Sosa told them, seeing heads nod.

"Money has been flowing like crazy," Twin said.

"Except on my block," Zels added, as they all looked at him, already knowing why.

"Nigga, your block on fire. I don't even drive through no more," Trill, who was Lil Hak's cousin stated.

"It's hard to get paper on a block that's hot. I have a resolution for you, Zels. Let's move your block to 9th and Shink?" Sosa said.

"That's the op block," said Twin, knowing the Outlaws hustled over there.

"I know." Sosa's smirk said it all.

"You want to take their block?" Lil Bean liked the sound of this idea.

"Yeah, because we're shutting 5th and Moore. We don't need that type of heat. We already got enough shit to deal with," Sosa said.

"Facts," Lil Hak said.

"I know what two buildings them niggas hustle from, so it shouldn't be hard to arrange some retaliation," Lez stated.

"Me and Lil Bean will put something together," Zels said, with him and Lil Bean being, the youngest and wildest of the crew.

"That's gonna be all bad," Big Lack said, knowing the city's body count was about to rise in a matter of hours.

"Since the FEDS in town, we have to move smarter and stay mindful, at least until they are full back," Sosa said.

"P. Cok will leave the county tomorrow. I know he is trying to run it up, so I'll have him with me in Wilson Projects or Badlands," said Twin.

"You know them Puerto Ricans hate us over there," Sosa stated, remembering what he did to Evil, years ago. When word got out that a Sosa Gang nigga killed Evil, people had a dislike for Sosa Gang over there. Sosa didn't have a clue how niggas knew he killed Evil. Block was the only one who knew, besides the fact that Sosa wore Evil's chain everywhere.

The Puerto Ricans in Badlands made it clear they wanted no problem with Sosa Gang whatsoever, and they left it at that.

"Leave Badlands alone. We don't need that area. It will be too much of a headache. Plus, our enemy right now is only the Outlaws. Everybody else is in their lane," Lil Hak said.

"You're right," Lez added.

"Everybody's product is bagged up in duffle bags next door, so until we meet again, the city is ours," Sosa said, popping a bottle of expensive Moet. Everybody else did the same thing.

***

West Philly

Dawgg went to his sister's crib to get his hair braided and to chill with her, since he had been busy hustling and staying alive.

"I never see you anymore," Foxy told him, putting his hair in box braids.

"You know how this shit be here, sis. Facts."

Sosa Gang

"I heard it's crazy over there in Tasker Projects. I been seeing it on the news almost every night. And Diesel's murder was big," Foxy said, really worried about his safety because the city was a war zone. Foxy had never seen so many murders in such a short amount of time.

"It's them bitch ass Sosa Gang niggas. They been going hard on us, ever since Frank's death. They been at us, and we been at them. This shit never gonna end, Foxy."

"Is Lez in the middle of it?" Foxy asked, wanting to know if her ex-boyfriend had anything to do with all this drama.

"No, it's mainly the young bulls. They roll with him, but Lez is one of the top members," Dawgg said, thinking back to how Lez used to treat him like a brother.

"Foxy, in the heat of war, none of that shit matters. If I see him, I slide on him."

"Dawgg, you need to grow the fuck up. Look at all your friends dying. You really trying to be next out here, with a fucking candle light party?" She shouted at him.

"Foxy, I'm too deep in this shit, and I'ma ride for my niggas." Dawgg saw she was done with his hair and got up.

"Whatever."

"You need some bread?" Dawgg pulled out a wad of money.

"No, I'm good, but you need to go see mommy," Foxy told him, checking her social media.

"I will tonight. Hit you later tonight." Dawgg picked up his colt 45 with a 30 shot clip.

"I love you and stay alive."

"Big facts. I won't let these niggas RIP me out in this bitch."

"You better not," she added, hoping he was right.

***

Temple University College, Philly

Karlee did her class assignment in med class on mitochondrial analysis and arteries in the human body.

She felt a vibration on her phone that was in her lap.

Seeing the *I miss you* text from Sean made her heart race. He did something to her that no man had ever done, and that was show real affection.

Having sex wit him took Karlee to another world. Her coochie hadn't stopped throbbing yet. She couldn't wait to get some dick. Karlee had started to feel like a sex addict off of one night of good loving.

After class, Karlee went to grab a bite to eat.

"Excuse me, are you Karlee?" A beautiful woman asked, approaching her in the hallway.

"Yes, I am. Who are you?"

"Sean's sister, I saw your pic last week. He spent a whole day talking about you," Zarhya said smiling.

"You must be Zarhya. He told me so much about you. Wow, it's nice to meet you." Karlee was excited.

"Same here. What are you about to do? I was gonna head to Subway."

"I was gonna grab a bite to eat, also. I'll come with you then." Karlee followed her new friend to the lot so they could get lunch and build.

Chapter 12

South Philly

Twin shared a fly ass apartment with his sister on 24th and Morris, in the cut. His sister, Traina, was the female him.

"Traina," Twin yelled, coming out of the back room.

"What? I'm busy," Traina said, doing her hair, getting dolled up for a big party tonight at a club uptown for the rapper Meek Mill and his crew.

"Look at you, little thot," Twin joked with her.

"Boy, please keep your bad energy in the back, hater."

"Where are you going?"

"Out with the girls to that rapper nigga's party. I heard it's gonna be lit, so I'm pulling up with Chyn, Tai, Liea, Moncia, and Chanella."

"Ayo, see what's up with Chyn. I heard she got some fire, pussy," said Twin, sitting on the couch, waiting for Zels to come thru.

"Twin, she don't want you, bruh. Chyn don't like drug dealers. Plus, she got a boyfriend, some dude from New Jersey, who owns a truck company," she told her brother.

He laughed. "All your friends be fucking with broke niggas."

"No, all my friends fuck with dudes who won't be going to jail." She gave him a look, before rolling her eyes.

"Whatever, goofy. Fuck them stank bitches." Twin heard a knock at the door and went to answer it.

"I called you early," Zels said, walking into the living room to see Traina, who looked so good he didn't recognize her. Traina looked at him and smiled.

"Hey, Zels," Traina said, seeing the handsome young man from time to time.

"You look nice, Traina," said Zels.

"Thanks, so do you."

"Don't gas her, Zels," Twin yelled from the kitchen.

"You can't gas a bad bitch," she shot back.

"Come on, Zels." Twin walked to the backroom.

"I'ight, Traina, nice seeing you."

"Hope to see you soon," she flirted. He caught on but walked it off.

Traina loved thugs, unlike her boujee friends, and Zels name in the street was nothing to fuck with. That turned her on, but she knew he and Twin were close, so Traina never crossed the line.

"You're the only person she is nice to. I think she's feeling you," Twin said joking.

"Nah, she just cool, bull."

"Bro, I see the way y'all look at each other."

"Cut it out, bro, you trippin'." Zels laughed it off, but he really had a crush on Traina.

"I will, but what's up you and Lil Beans? Are you ready for y'all movie?" Twin asked.

"Facts. I just left West Philly, and we came up with some simple shit to do at 12 p.m. when the police do shift change," Zels told Twin, not trying to give too much detail on the event planned to take place in a few hours.

"You got whoever's gonna run the block prepared for what could be in store?"

"I'm running on one corner, and letting Slick run the other corner," Zels said, already figuring it out.

"That's smart. You need me to slide? I ain't got shit to do," Twin asked.

"We sliding with enough young bulls." Zels got up to leave as Twin walked him out a Traina waved bye to Zels and flicked Twin her middle finger.

***

South, Philly

The hood was jumping tonight. On 9th and Shink, hustlers filled the streets, selling all types of drugs. Cars blasted music late at night, not giving a fuck about the civilians living there.

68

Grammy and Biggie controlled the long strip. They were down with the famous Outlaws.

"Ayo, Grammy, you heard about that Meek Mill party uptown?" Deonate asked. One of Grammy's workers approach the front of the building, where ten niggas surrounded, as they did twenty-four seven.

"Yeah, niggas heard about that shit, but I ain't got time to be a sitting duck," Grammy said, referring to the ops, who always were in the club, looking for smoke.

"Biggie and them niggas talking about sliding up there, when that shit gets jumping," Deonate said, as Grammy blew his weed smoke in the kid's face.

"So go with Biggie fat ass. We getting money tonight. It's the first of the month, cuz," Grammy told Deonate, as three vans creeped up on both ends of the block.

"Grammy, who that?" Crime said, before the mayhem started.

Tat. Tat. Tat. Tat. Tat. Tat. Tat. Tat. Tat. Tat. Tat. Tat. Tat. Tat. Tat. Tat.

Grammy tried to run in the building, but Lil Bean's bullets riddled his lower back, making his skinny body slam into the building's front door. Three of Grammy's soldiers fought back, bullet for bullet, but there were 13 shooters, with all assault rifles.

Legs and arms started to get shot off before Grammy's crew all laid on the ground, fighting for their lives, if they weren't already a goner.

***

Down the block, Biggie and four of his shooters ducked behind cars, hiding from the gunmen, after seeing five of Biggie's foot soldiers laid out dead.

Zels and two shooters creeped up to the cars Biggie and his boys hid behind. Managing to climb on top of the car roofs; they all had a clean shot of their targets.

Biggie was praying on the ground, as he looked up to see Zels on top of the car. Biggie had no bullets left in his gun.

"I was gonna let you work for my crew, but that would be ide-alistic and pragmatic, seeing you just killed two of my young bulls," Zels said.

"That wasn't me, bruh. Let's get this money together. I always wanted to be down with y'all," Biggie said in a shaky voice, slowly reaching for a 9mm on the curb next to him, which belonged to one of his dead homies.

"I see you reaching, fat boy, but too slow," Zels said before lighting Biggie's ass up with bullets.

Zels' crew killed the rest of Biggie's niggas, as he looked down the block to see Lil Bean and his team were driving away, as sirens could be heard.

"Time to move," Zels yelled, hopping off the car, seeing two Sosa Gang niggas dead on the ground. As he ran back to the van with an AR-15 in his hand, cars drove by, scared to death. One of the cars was Traina in a Range Rover filled with chicks, all scared, except her.

Traina gave Zels a wink, before racing off, trying not to get caught up in no mass shooting shit on her way to the club.

Lil Beans and Zels met up in North Philly to give a local chop shop back the vans they borrowed for $10,000. Everybody went to lay low for the night because the city had police all over, looking for vans.

Chapter 13

CFCF Jail, Philly

Crispy left the jail, after visiting his cousin, Burn, who'd just got sentenced to 71 years in prison for a murder Crispy committed last year. Since his cousin stood strong and didn't snitch, Crispy planned to ride his long bid out with him, no matter the cost.

Last night, Crispy and Sin lost a lot of men in a big shootout in South Philly. Rumors had it, Zels and Lil Bean were seen at the shootout, so he already knew what was up.

Sin called him earlier, setting up a get together at his crib so they could talk, and it was time they re-up anyway.

In the past month, he had been losing a lot of money, due to the fear his ops were causing. Regardless, he knew this was a part of the game he loved and signed up for.

Crispy drove past a Lexus LC 500 to see Twin driving, bopping his head to music, heading into the jail.

"Ain't this a bitch," Crispy said, waiting for the Lexus to get further down the block before he made a U-turn and tailed him from a distance.

***

Today, P. Cok was being released, and Twin made sure he pulled up on time to pick his boy up.

P. Cok repped South and West Philly. He had been getting big money with their gang since a young bull, so the crew had love for him.

Twin parked in the visitor's parking lot and got out of his new Lexus, which he liked to stunt in. Twin woke up to the news of how Zels and Lil Bean did them niggas on 9th and Shink, which made him realize he was glad to be on the right team.

The news report made it seem as if a bunch of terrorists killed all those people, but they did say it was most likely a turf war.

Twin walked inside the main entrance, where inmates were normally released and posted up on the wall, as correctional officers went in and out, some starting their shift, while others were ending their shifts, or about to do a double.

P. Cok walked out with a small bag in his hand, his long beard shining, and a smile, happy to be free.

"As-Salaam-Alaikum," P. Cok said.

"Wa-Alaikum-Salaam," Twin greeted back, giving his boy a hug.

"Man, your name is heavy in the jail. We basically run that shit."

"I heard, bro. We litty right now. The city is ours," Twin stated, knowing P. Cok was missing in action because of his two-year bid in jail.

"Niggas killed a bunch of niggas on 9th and Shink last night. Shit is all over the news, bull," P. Cok said, as Twin laughed.

They talked, unaware of the man inside the Nissan, watching them.

About twenty feet away from Twin's car, there was a scream, which made both men look behind them.

Bloc. Block. Bloc. Bloc. Bloc. Bloc. Bloc. Bloc. Bloc. Bloc. Bloc. Bloc. Bloc. Bloc. Bloc.

The 9 mm Luger SXT backed into the parking lot, as P. Cok caught two in his chest and one in his neck.

Twin was quick on his feet, running to the car to get his gun. He saw Crispy dash off, as correctional officers were running out of the jail entrance to see what was going on.

Crispy pulled off. Twin wanted to chase him, but instead, he went to P. Cok, whose eyes were still open, as he was losing a lot of blood out of his neck and chest.

"Look out for my mom and daughter, ock," P. Cok said, before his eyes rolled into the back of his head.

The jail nurses came out to help and save P. Cok, but it was pointless. He had no pulse. Cops came and asked Twin what happened, all he replied to them was he didn't see anything.

Sosa Gang

Driving back to South Philly, the thought of Crispy killing P. Cok played every second in his mind.

***

West Philly

Lez and Big Lack were at a car dealership, picking out a new car for them both, on Lez behalf.

"You see Lil Hak's new Mercedes, cap?" Big Lack asked, looking at a row of Porsches.

"His car is fly as shit, cuz. I can't lie, that's why I'm about to step my game up today," Lez said, walking over to all the new Audi's.

"Oh shit, cuz," Big Lack said in shock, as he read a text from one of his boys.

"What happened now?"

"They just killed P. Cok in front of CFCF jail, bro."

"Twin went to pick him up, right?" Lez remembered Twin saying something about him coming home.

"Facts. I'm calling Twin." Big Lack called Twin, who picked up on the last ring.

"Ayo," Twin said.

"Are you straight?" Big Lack asked.

"Yeah, I'm getting with y'all later, bull," Twin said, before hanging up, not in the mood to talk.

"Him and P. Cok were really close, so I know it touched his heart," Lez said.

"Facts."

"I am getting this," Lez said, looking at a new Porsche Panamera Turbo S, worth over $170,000.

"Damn, I'll get this Audi truck," Big Lack said. They waved over a salesman to get the paperwork ready so they could leave the lot with the cars paid and full.

***

Downtown Philly

Sosa popped up on Karlee to take her out to catch a movie at a movie theater near her college.

"I have not seen you in a few days. Where you have been at, babe?"

"Busy," Sosa said.

"Too busy for me, huh?"

"Never too busy for a queen like you."

"Smooth, playa," she laughed.

"How school?"

"I passed some important exam with flying colors. Guess who I met yesterday, and we had a long talk?"

"Who?"

"Zarhya"

"Oh yeah, I forgot to introduce y'all two. I'm sorry, babe," he stated.

"She's really sweet and caring."

"And spoiled."

"I saw that in her," Karlee said, seeing a Chevrolet Corvette being pulled over.

"She's a good girl, though," Sosa said, seeing his brother's Chevrolet surrounded by a bunch of police cars. Sosa saw keys of coke and a gun on the trunk of Block's car, and he was in handcuffs.

"Babe, look at all that coke," Karlee said.

"I know." Sosa drove by, thinking if he should call his dad. But he knew Block had a lawyer on retainer for times like this.

74

Chapter 14

Darby, PA

There was a small party at Sin's house, with a bunch of women running around out back, making their own pool party with water guns, turning up.

Sin, Crispy, and Dawgg all were inside the basement, pouring drinks and discussing business.

"I'm sure we all know what's going on here," Sin said, sitting in his La-Z-Boy.

"I came so close to killing Twin this morning, but I got P. Cok," Crispy started, taking a sip of Henny.

"P. Cok would have been a problem, so that's good to hear," Sin told him.

"Them niggas killed Biggie and Grammy at the same fucking time. But the crazy part is they moved in on 9th and Shink," Dawgg said.

"Who?" Crispy asked.

"Sosa Gang niggas took over 9th and Shink. It's like twenty of them little niggas over there right now," Dawgg said.

"It's cool," Sin said calmly.

"Hell naw, it ain't. We can't let them take our block," Crispy told Sin.

"Relax, I have a plan. Let them have that block and holla at Status from Badlands. They fuck with us," Sin said.

"I don't think this is smart, Sin," Crispy said.

"The higher ups called me this morning and informed me of some matters that are more important than a block. Everybody play it cool, and let's get back to focusing on the paper," Sin said.

"I feel like we lost, and I dislike losing," Dawgg stated.

"Neither do I, young bull. We're gonna be just fine," Crispy said.

"I got the drop on Lil Hak. One of my eaters is his main jint, so I plan to slide on him myself," said Sin.

"Take some shooters," Dawgg told him.

"Nah, I got this," Sin smiled.

"What time is the product gonna be ready, cuz? I have to make a couple of plays in York and Allentown tonight," Crispy asked.

"It should be there in the morning at the regular spots. I tried to push for tonight, but the plug is in Chicago right now," Sin told them.

"I'ight just hit me. I gotta bounce," Crispy said, as Dawgg followed, leaving Sin thinking about his next move.

***

Southwest Philly

Lil Hak had Pam's legs in the air, as he long stroked her wet pussy and she glanced up moaning with sensual pleasure.

"Ohhhh, yes, fuck meee," Pam yelled, holding on to his back.

Lil Hak sucked on her breasts, teasing her nipples, as she shuddered every time he pounded out the bottom of Pam's little cunt.

"Who pussy is this, bitch?" Lil Hak gritted, as he picked up the pace.

"Uggghhhh, yourssss," she yelled, coming and making a mess on her Fendi sheets with her copious juices.

"I want to fuck you from behind," Lil Hak said, changing positions.

"Wait. Lil Hak, I have something I gotta tell you. Please don't hit me?" Pam said, with tears in her eyes.

"What the fuck you crying for?" Lil Hak hoped she hadn't caught any STDs and given it to him, or some crazy shit like that, because they did have an open relationship.

"I really fucked up," she said, looking out the hotel window, as if she ordered some food.

"What?"

"I was fucking with some guy named Sin, and he paid me twenty thousand to give him this location. He said to fuck you for an hour, then leave so he could come in here to talk to you," she said.

"Bitch, you can't be serious."

"I'm sorry. I felt bad so I had to tell you," she cried.

Lil Hak rushed to get dressed and picked up his 357 Rem Max handgun, staying low. He thought about popping Pam, but she wasn't worth the bullet, at least not yet.

"What car is he in?" Lil Hak asked, peeking out the window into the parking lot full of cars.

"A blue Jeep with tints," she said.

Lil Hak saw the Jeep a few cars away from Pam's Honda Civic.

Lil Hak ran out of the hotel, like superman, heading towards the blue Jeep.

Boom. Boom. Boom.

Sin climbed out of the Jeep, caught off guard by Lil Hak's ambush. In five more minutes, he was about to run up in the room on him and Pam, to kill them

Sin fired back with a double barrel shotgun, putting holes the size of basketballs in the cars, but missing his target.

"What the fuck is that?" Lil Hak shouted, ducking behind a car.

"Don't hide killer," Sin yelled shooting out the windows of the car next to Lil Hak.

Boom. Boom.

Lil Hak fired but missed by a long shot. He was trying to get away from the shotgun and get a good shot with the few bullets he had left.

Sin couldn't see where Lil Hak went, as he stood in the middle of the lot, trying to find his opponent.

Boom. Boom.

"Fuck," Sin yelled in pain, getting grazed in his left shoulder as Lil Hak ran off with no more bullets.

Sin fired, but Lil Hak was already out of the parking lot.

Civilians started to peep their heads out of their windows, once the shooting died down, calling the police. Sin dipped, in his bag about fucking up a once in a lifetime move.

***

"Are you ready to talk yet, or do we call your ride to the county jail? I hate to break it to you, but we just found six more keys in your stash spot," Officer Spoon said, as he entered the interrogation room.

"Six?"

"Yeah. Plus, another pistol, my favorite kind, a Glock 22."

"Man, that shit not mine," Block yelled, never in his life owning a Glock 22.

"It is now, unless you're willing to help us to save yourself."

"I'm no rat."

"Alpo wasn't either, nor Sammy the bull, but when a nigga under pressure, anything goes. It's you or them," Officer Spoon said, sitting down.

"A'ight if I gave you some names, how much time will I have to do?"

"Depending on how good the cases are, you won't have to do a day."

"My plug, and the middleman, Sosa."

"Sosa? You mean Sosa Gang?" Officer Spoon asked.

"No, the kid's name is Sosa, and the biggest dealer in Philly is Barry. I know all about them," Block said, snitching on his dad and brother.

"Oh, this is gonna be juicy. Hold on, let me get some coffee and a snake," Officer Spoon said, leaving the room for a second.

Chapter 15

West Philly

"Roll that shit up, bro," Lil Bean told his cousin, Chainz, as they posted up at 49th and Lancaster.

"Nigga, fuck all dat shit. I'm taking this with me to Princess crib," Chainz said, waiting for his client to arrive so he could sell him the two hundred grams in his shorts.

"You still on that, though?"

"That's wifey, bro, don't disrespect me."

"Nigga, fuck outta here. Shawty fucked the whole gang, bro." Lil Bean looked at Chainz like he'd lost his mind.

"That's her past life."

"I'ight, I just saw her in South Philly, fucking Trend and Bossy."

"You lying."

"She not my bitch, why I need to lie? And they say shawty burning."

"Princess a good chick."

"Damn, cuz, Princess burned you before, huh?"

"Just twice," Chainz admitted.

Lil Bean started dying laughing, as a car pulled up to the curb.

"You goofy, I think this is my client," Chainz said, approaching the car.

Chainz didn't recognize the car, but his clients would pull up in all types of cars to cop work from Chainz and his crew.

The dark tint was up when Chainz got to the window, so he tapped on the glass. Lil Bean peeped something strange about the car. A fiend would have been thirsty to get his or her hit and quick to unlock the door of the Toyota.

Three doors opened and gunmen all jumped out firing.

Boc. Boc. Boc. Boc. Boc. Boc. Boc. Boc. Boc. Boc. Boc. Boc. Boc. Boc.

He took out another man, while the last one crawled under the Toyota, trying to shoot at Lil Bean's feet or legs.

A dirt bike sped down the block and Lil Bean didn't pay it no mind as he watched the last shooter trying to get his Draco.

The man on the dirt bike popped a wheelie, aiming a tech 9 at Lil Bean, who caught a glimpse of it too late.

Tat. Tat. Tat. Tat. Tat. Tat. Tat. Tat. Tat. Tat. Tat. Tat. Tat. Tat. Tat. Tat. Tat. Tat. Tat. Tat. Tat.

Dawg killed Lil Bean and rode off, leaving his shooter on the block, hiding under a car.

***

Uptown Philly

Ten minutes ago, Block had called Sosa, asking him to meet up with him at a Wal-Mart parking lot.

Sosa remembered the last time he saw Block; his brother was getting arrested. Sosa saw the drugs and gun with his own eyes.

Sosa asked his dad if Block had contacted him, and Barry told him no. The last time he talked to Block was yesterday, and Sosa found that strange.

Sosa pulled into the parking lot, trying to make sense of how the fuck Block got out so quick.

Block was sitting inside of his car, the same one Sosa saw him get arrested in. Normally, when a nigga got locked up with drugs and weapons in their car, the police would impound the whip.

Getting out of the Maserati, he peeped Block hanging up his phone.

"Bro, what's the vibe with you? How's everything?" Block started with a nervous look.

"Same ol' shit, bull."

"You need some work?" Block asked, out of the blue.

Sosa was blindsided by that. "No. I'm good, bro."

"You sure? I got you whenever. Shit been real busy. I been getting this outta town money," Block bragged.

"That's where you've been?" Sosa asked, playing the game, seeing how far Block was about to go with his lies.

Sosa Gang

"I been in Pittsburgh for a week now."

"Since when you started fucking around out there? Them niggas don't play fair."

"I got some clients out there, bro. but how is the work moving for you?" Block asked, as he looked around the parking lot.

"Call me later, bro. I have to go check on my young bull. He broke his neck this morning." Sosa checked his phone, not feeling Block's energy. Something was very off.

"Love you, bro," Block said, waiting for a reply.

Sosa got in his truck, leaving, with no reply.

***

South Philly

Donny left work from working on the city's garbage trucks. That was the job he had been at for a decade.

Unlike his brother, Sin, he loved a regular life, working a nice job, trying to stay out the way.

Donny wanted to stop and get his girl some flowers for her birthday, which was today. He felt like she deserved the best.

The flower shop next to 16th and Catherine was opening, so he pulled over and rushed inside.

"Can I get some red roses?" Donny asked the Spanish woman.

"How many would you like?"

"Two dozen."

"Somebody gonna feel special today," she said, going to the back so she could sell him fresh flowers.

After getting the flowers, Donny knew his baby's mother would love the flowers and be appreciative.

Walking outside, Donny saw somebody leaning on his car, smoking a blunt."

"That's my car," Donny said.

"So what?" Twin stated.

"Man, look, I don't want no problems, bro," Donny stated.

"Too late for all of that. You're already in it, bro. You're Sin's brother," Twin stated, looking him in his eyes.

"I don't fuck with Sin. His problems isn't mines. You gotta take that up with him."

"I'm sorry, cuz, but this is the game, young bull." Twin pulled out the gun.

Boc. Boc. Boc.

Twin gave him headshots, then walked off, leaving Donny there dead.

Sosa Gang

Chapter 16

Gee laid in his cell on the bed, waiting for his visit. He was listening to a State Property album, bopping his head to the beat.

Looking at the calendar on his wall, he was marking down month from month, until his release date.

Being in jail was like a life within itself, the gossip, killing, fighting, drug use, rats, and of course, the snake shit that comes with it.

Yesterday, there was a one-on-one fight in the gym with Trouble, from his crew, and Bounty, from the Outlaws. Gee wasn't too happy about that because he knew that it could lead to more things, but they both shook hands after.

Gee got a letter from Lez today, and a money order from Sosa for five bands. He appreciated the love and loyalty his boys had for him.

"Ayo, Gee," he heard someone yelling his name down the tier, as he jumped off the bed with is shoes already on.

"What's up?" Gee peeped his head out of his cell to see a gang of niggas from his crew rushing up to him.

"Shit lit, bro. Niggas just humped Trouble on the other side of the spot, bull," Tatted Mike said, dressed up with a coat and scurf, ready for war.

"Are we sliding? Y'all strapped up?" Gee said, as six niggas pulled out big knives with strings tied to the ends.

"Everybody ready, bull. It's like ten of them clowns on the lower tier," Jumping stated.

"We out then," Gee said, running down the stairs, leading the pack.

On the lower level, they saw the group of Outlaw niggas laughing and talking about how Trouble got put in the hospital.

When one of them saw Sosa Gang pull up with knives, he smoothly slid in his cell, before the shit popped off.

Gee stabbed the first nigga he saw in the head, then it went up. Tatted Mike stabbed three of them, as the rest of Sosa Gang put in work.

The Outlaws were screaming and running from that knife work, until the correctional officers ran onto the tier, hitting everybody with sticks and pepper spray. Everybody from the fight ended up on lock up.

***

West Philly

Twin and Lez parked parallel next to each other outside of a Philly cheesesteak spot, next to Taco Bell, on 52nd and Martin.

Lez had just come from dropping off some coke in Westparks projects to his boy Wezzy.

"You heard what happened," Twin said, parking his car.

"I just dropped off ten bands to Lil Bean's mom and sister," Lez stated, in his bag.

"I hit Sin's brother yesterday for that, so I know bro finna feel that shit, cuz," said Twin, pulling out a cig to blow.

"These niggas caught my young bull slipping, bro," Lez said, sick about the news.

"We're gonna get back, bro. Regardless, we are still up on the scoreboard," Twin added.

"For now, bro. But I gotta slide off real quick, cuz. You straight?"

"Facts." Twin knew Lil Bean was like a brother to him, so it hit home.

Officer Kilow walked into the office, after fucking a stripper bitch he dealt with from time to time. She was also his special informant.

She kept him hipped to all the info in the streets and this morning, she'd told him about the crazy beef between Sosa Gang and the Outlaws.

"Kilow, step in my office," Captain Torres said, seeing Kilow come out of the office with the coffee mug he'd had for years.

"What's happening, boss man? You've been out sick for two weeks. I missed your stank breath ass," Kilow joked with his boss.

"Cut the dumb shit, homo. Now look, peep game, the FBI, DEA, and ATF have been on us about this turf war between these kids," Captain Torres said looking through some paperwork.

"The Outlaws and Sosa Gang members, correct?" Kilow asked, already on point.

"Yeah, you sharp. I need you to go undercover on either side because these kids are out here moving some serious weight. The body count has been crazy, and something needs to be done."

"I understand. Do you have photos?" Kilow asked, so he could be familiar with who the top dogs were.

"Yeah. It's all right here. This is for you. Now get the fuck out my office, rookie," Captain Torres joked, picking up his work phone to call the DEA office, so he could let them know his people were on the case.

"Fuck you, bastard." Kilow walked out, making his detour to the small booth he worked in.

When he went to his desk, Kilow flipped through the folder to see pictures of Crispy, Dawgg, and Sin. Then he opened the next side to see Lil Bean, Zels, Lil Hak, Twin and Big Lack. But when he saw, Lez his heart stopped.

He knew Lez fucked with Sosa Gang, but not to the point where he would be considered one of the main leaders.

Kilow thought about the family cook-out his family was having this coming weekend and figured it would be the right time to bring the situation up to Lez. Kilow saw that the Sosa Gang crew was responsible for over twenty-five murders in the past two years. He couldn't believe it.

***

Downtown, Philly

Last month, Lez had copped a nice little condo in an upscale, white people area. He'd recently moved his new girl, Valeria, in with him. She was a sexy, pretty, brown skin dime.

Valeria spent most of her days shopping and spending his money. Lez wasn't used to letting a woman milk him, whether he had it or not.

True, she had some good pussy and was a bad bitch, but Valeria was starting to become a headache. Lez was trying to find a way to get his revenge for Lil Bean's death.

"Hey, boo boo," Valeria walked in with shopping bags.

"Hi, you home early." Lez looked at her and her phat pussy print flexing through her leggings.

"I need more money."

"What? I just gave you money." Lez thought it was a joke.

"Babe, shit so expensive."

"I'm not giving you any more paper. Relax for the day."

"I know what you need, a good blow job," she said, about to get on her knees.

"I got a better ideal. Get the fuck out my crib," he said.

"What? You serious?"

"Get the fuck out." Lez grabbed her by her hair and dragged her to the door, as she yelled that he would regret this.

Chapter 17

Downtown Philly

"I can't believe you really took me to the art museum baby," Karlee said, holding Sosa's hand, looking at the paintings of famous people, drawn by well-known artists.

"We gotta do this once a month because it's some nice work here. I never really looked at art the way I'm looking at it now," Sosa told her, looking at a picture with a naked woman and clouds surrounding her.

"You know why I love coming here?"

"Why babe?" Sosa knew Karlee loved art galleries, and events like this.

"Because you can take a look into what other people think and feel. Some people can only express themselves through art, words, poems, and paintings."

"It's hard to look into someone's life just by their art."

"Not really. You just gotta relate to it," Karlee said, shrugging her shoulders.

"Have you ever tried to paint or draw?" Sosa asked, trying to get to know her more.

Sosa was really into Karlee. She had morals and values most women failed to have these days.

"No, but I do have a secret I used to do as a hobby," she blushed.

"Oh, you gotta tell me."

"No, Sean. You gonna clown me. I know you are, baby."

"No. I'm not."

"You sure?"

"Yeah."

"Ok, I used to rap when I was younger. I used to think I was the next Mc Lite," she said.

"Not you. I can't even imagine that shit." He wanted to laugh because she would never strike him as that type. Karlee reminded him of a black girl, raised in a white area, surrounded by all white people, who turned her out.

"My mom is still telling me how I used to run around the house rapping all day." She laughed, thinking back to when she was a little girl.

"Spit something for me?"

"Boy, no."

"Come on, girl. I know you still got it," he joked, hoping to hear her go into a bar real fast.

"Sean, that was years ago."

"You're just scared to tell the truth," he said, trying to gas her up.

"Maybe later, but I'm hungry. Lots of people go to that steak house next to Hampton Inn?" Karlee asked, holding his arm.

"Ok, let's slide because I ain't eat shit all day."

"Yes, you did."

"No, dead ass, I didn't"

"You ate my pussy this morning," she giggled, seeing him shake his head at how nasty she was.

Since they'd recently moved in together, things between them were amazing. With Karlee having to be at school most of the time, Sosa spent most of his days running around.

"I'ma eat it again tonight."

"Feel free to, please."

"My pleasure," he said, as they walked out of the art gallery.

"I know you love when I blow in that pussy, while sucking on the clit." He saw her face light up brightly.

"Oh my God, you crazy, baby." Karlee felt her pussy getting drenched.

"Where do you see us in five years, babe?" Sosa switched up the question.

"I love how you can talk nasty, then get straight to business," Karlee told him, loving how he was so versatile with his speech and conversation.

The other night, they'd talked about a book called *The 5 Love Languages,* and the one they carried.

Karlee expressed that she loved gifts as her love language, and Sosa's was words, because a nice word could make a person's heart melt.

As they walked down the stairs to his truck, Sosa saw a car pulling out a few cars behind.

"You're a gentleman," Karlee said, as Sosa opened the door for her.

"I try." Sosa's focus was on the car as he walked around the truck, and then it all happened so fast.

Two gunmen and Sin jumped out with no masks, but Sosa was on point. Before the two shooters aimed, Sosa was already on them.

Bloc. Bloc. Bloc. Bloc. Bloc.

Sin saw the movement and ducked behind the car, after seeing his men drop to the ground.

Boc. Boc. Boc.

Sin fired at Sosa, who dipped behind an Acura, trying to get away from his truck so nobody would hit Karlee.

Cops could be heard, and Sosa saw Sin get back in the car, pulling off. He did the same, speeding off, almost hitting cars in the process of driving.

"You ok, babe?" Sosa said, forgetting for a second she was even in there.

"Can we just switch cars and go get some steak, please," Karlee shot back calmly, as if the shootout didn't faze her one bit.

"Ok. I'm sorry."

"For what? I know what I signed up for, Sean. I'm far from green, love." She looked through the rearview mirror, glad no cops were chasing them.

"That's a ride or die," Sosa laughed, turning up the radio.

***

Southwest Philly

Pam had just been dropped off by one of her sugar daddies at her mom's house on 72nd and Paschell. It was two a.m., and she was drained from fucking all night.

When Only Fans on social media wasn't paying the bills, she would sell pussy to some old white men she would meet online.

She walked to the end of the hall, hoping Mama Love was sleep because she hated people coming in her house late at night.

Pam had no remorse for setting up Lil Hak for all that money. But she felt like, without her telling him, he would have been dead, so he should have sent a thank you card, or more.

The whole city knew about the Sosa Gang and Outlaws beef, and there was a lot of money on the line.

Pam tip-toed inside the dark crib, taking off her sneakers, walking through the living room, unable to see anything because her contacts were not in.

"Look at you, sneaky bitch," a familiar voice said, stopping her where she stood.

"Lil Hak, hey, baby," she said, as the lights came on. Pam saw her mom was tied to a chair, with a dish rag in her mouth, tied down by a rope.

"Bitch, you played me good, but it's my turn now," Lil Hak spit.

"Just let my mom go, please," Pam begged.

"Where Sin at?" Lil Hak approached her.

"Sin's baby mother is my best friend. She works at H&M, that clothing store in Chester. Her name is Bianca."

"Thank you, so helpful," Lil Hak said, looking at his two goons and nodding his head.

Boom. Boom.

Pam watched the men shoot her mama in her legs, before Lil Hak aimed his gun at her face.

Boc. Boc. Boc. Boc. Boc.

Pam's blood squirted on his face. He wiped it off and shot Pam twice more, going into overkill.

***

Sosa Gang

Green County Prison, PA

Gee hated the SHU. Being in the box made him think and focus on himself. The riot that popped off sent three people to the hospital. One of the Outlaws was still fighting for his life on life support. Gee had stabbed him first, so he'd been praying the fuck nigga pulled through because he wasn't trying to fight no jail house body.

His boys, Bea and Josh, sent word they were waiting for him to come out the box to see if they wanted to finish up because Trouble was pronounced dead four days ago.

A correctional officer came to his door. He was a big white cracker, who hated all black people with a passion.

"You gonna be the one to take that murder charge, NIGGA," the C.O. said up close to the door, so only Gee could hear.

Gee learned from brothers, who had been down a long time in the prison, to stay away from the guards and never talk back, or they would rush into the cell to try to break your jaw, rib, or even kill you.

"You ain't gotta talk back. I'll be waiting for you, bitch box. Now get ready for your fucking visit." The cop spit on the glass and walked off.

Gee took a deep breath and got ready for his visit, thinking how he could never risk his freedom again and come back.

***

Gee was walking to his visit in cuffs and shackles, with two guards on his side. In the visiting room, Gee was placed behind a glass because he was in the SHU, and box inmates had booth glass visits.

Shierka, his beautiful sister, sat on the other side of the glass smiling, happy to see him. When he wrote her, he was saying some shit had popped off.

"I miss you, ugly. What happened? Why are you in cuffs?" Shierka asked.

"The ops," he replied.

She knew who Gee referred to.

"Come on, Gee. You on your way home. Fuck that dumb shit. I need you out here, bro," she cried.

"Don't cry sis. It's a part of the game. I will be ok. I'ma be home in no time."

"You better, I swear."

"I heard you got a good job now?"

"Yeah, at a group home, making almost twenty-three an hour," she boasted.

"Damn. Get money, then," he replied, as they talked about future plans.

Chapter 18

West Philly

Malcolm X Park was packed with Lez's family reunion, which they did every year around this time. Over three hundred people showed up from all over Philly, and other states.

Lez forgot how much family he really had because he didn't really fuck with them as much. Lil Hak was on his way to the park because he had to take care of some business down the street.

The beef in the city had been litty still, but it'd been dying down for the past week, which was cool. But any second, shit could get crazy.

When Sosa told him about the shootout with Sin, he couldn't believe it because nobody really knew Sosa, especially as their shot caller.

Now Sosa was exposed. His outlook changed. The circumstances became different. And he was ready to turn up. Hearing Sosa plan an invasion last night was the funniest shit because he had a real drawing board for some extraordinary killing shit that the gang would've never been able to put together on their own, without him.

Valeria had been blowing up his phone, trying her best to get him back, but it was bad timing. He had to let her sweat, so she'd know better next time.

Lez saw his brother walking up to him with a picture of his dead sister on his shirt.

Every day, he thought about how Eva wasn't here anymore, and it made him want to go crazy on the Outlaws, but he knew in due time.

"Lez, how have you been?" Kilow asked, drinking a beer, sitting on the bench, as music filled the park and the smell of bar-b-que flooded the air.

"Chilling, my nigga," Lez responded.

Kilow and Lez had no type of bond, since they were teenagers. They grew apart and went on two different paths in life.

"I saw you at Eva's funeral and I wanted to holla at you, but we both were emotionally fucked up," Kilow stated.

"Facts, bro."

"I found out who did it."

"Oh yeah?" Lez played dumb because he knew his brother was a cop and Lez kept his street dealings away from him.

"Don't play dumb with me, Lez. You know what's going on out here in the streets." Kilow started to get upset because Lez was trying to play him for a goofy.

"I don't know what the fuck you talking about, and today ain't the day, Officer Kilow," Lez said seriously, as Kilow chuckled.

"Let me tell you something, the city is a war zone, with your crew and the Outlaws."

"My crew? I don't—"

"Cut the bullshit. Your name is in the mix, Lez. You're listed as a West Philly Sosa Gang nigga. I got the caseload. My boss gave it to me so I can solve it. But luckily, he don't know you're my brother."

"So, you're gonna arrest me? Do you, cuz," Lez told him, not caring.

"It's bigger than me, young buck. You got the DEA and FBI on y'all ass."

"I realize there is no region with indefinite boundaries in the jungle, so you can't escape what you signed up for," Lez stated.

"Some things are indestructible, but you're not indecipherable to change, Lez. When these FEDS and DEA agents start running down, it's going to be too late." Kilow hoped Lez wasn't that naive where he would let his integrity for the streets take his life away.

"I stick to the code, Kilow."

"A code that's watered down and nobody follows no more. Remember that you're following a code that don't exist anymore."

"It may not have existence, but this is who I am, Kilow. You outta all people know that because it's in your heart," Lez told him.

"It's in my blood, not my heart," Kilow corrected him.

"I hear you, bro." Lez saw Lil Hak's car pull up in the lot.

"I'ma do what I can, Lez. But if I was you, I would change up my dealings." Kilow walked off, seeing Lil Hak coming towards Lez. He knew who Lil Hak was from the caseload he was studying day and night, trying to figure out a way to exclude his brother from what was coming.

"What's good, you West Philly nigga?" Lil Hak said walking up to him in a Gucci outfit, with shades to match.

"Same ole shit, cuz."

"Why the bad energy and sad face? I could've stayed at Trilla's crib for that," Lil Hak told him, seeing something was really under his skin. But everybody was exhausted right now, losing friends and family members to the streets, due to their beef.

"I be seeing the FEDS everywhere I look now, bro. We just gotta move more silent and militant."

"That's real, bro. I agree with that, cuz. The DEA just snatched up Press and Seen from Greenway this morning for a body from five years ago, so they fishing." Lil Hak knew, sooner or later, the law was going to get on their ass with body's dropping everywhere, and niggas getting away with it.

"Them niggas gonna hold it down? You got everything in order for this move?" Lez asked about the upcoming mission.

"Yeah, Trilla gonna be the driver."

"I'ight bet."

"Sosa told me Gee crashed out with the Outlaw niggas?" Lil Hak asked.

"Yeah, bro in da box."

"I can't wait until he touch. That was my little nigga." Lil Hak had love for Gee. He looked at him like a real brother.

"Bro family, but he'll be out soon."

"It's some bitches out here, cuz. I saw a chick with an ass so phat that shit looked like a punching bag," Lil Hak laughed.

"I don't know half of these people, cuz. That's why I'm sitting here, sipping lean, smoking weed, and watching," Lez stated.

"Well listen, cuz. I'm about to go get some food and try to fuck one of your cousins," Lil Hak joked, walking off. But he was serious, at the same time.

***

CFCF Jail, Philly

Wayne hung up the phone in the unit, after having a conversation with his lawyer, requiring the details of the next motion he planned to put in on his behalf.

Since being arrested on murder charges outside of a club, Wayne's life had never been the same.

Wayne was the leader of the D.C. crew. But since being in jail, his little brother, Roddy, had been holding shit down with the young boy, Kaba.

The case he had wasn't looking good because every time he turned around, a new witness was popping up, and a statement said Wayne killed them in front of the club, two years ago.

His girl, Abby, had been by his side since the first day, and he loved her sexy ass so much for that .Wayne would see people's loved ones turn on them within five days of their bid. And the crazy part of it was most of them were planning to go home and show them same ones love.

There was a few things about Wayne's case that he only knew, and refused to tell anyone else, because if he ever got ahead of him, Wayne wanted to kill him. Someone close to him sat up the whole shooting and sent niggas to kill Wayne that night, outside the club.

After killing two of the gunmen, he ran down on a gunman he'd shot but was still alive and asked the man who sent him. When he told Wayne who sent them, the feeling of betrayal hit Wayne's heart, and he cursed himself for giving the wrong people loyalty.

All he had been hearing about was Sosa Gang out there fucking the city up. Wayne and Lez had a little beef over a bitch back in the day, but that was a while ago.

In the jail, the SIS separated the Outlaws and Sosa Gang by placing each group in different units, because they were fighting and stabbing each other on sight.

Wayne went to his cell to take a nap. The inmates in the dayroom were loud and always doing the most.

"Ayo, Wayne," Fat Beats yelled, coming out of his cell.

"What's up, young bull?"

"Niggas killed my sister last week, cuz. Pam ain't do shit to nobody. The Chaplin told me this morning. I lost my phone privileges so I couldn't even call my fam." Fat Beats was a regular nigga from Southwest. He used to get a lot of money, which got him forty-five years in prison. He got sentenced last week.

"You know who did it?"

"Nah, man, but I bet it's that Lil Hak nigga. She told me about him in her last letter," he said.

"Damn, bull, you'll be ok. You just got sentenced. You about to go upstate. Just be easy and stay focused."

"Good looks, Wayne." Fat Beats went back in his cell.

Wayne felt the nigga's pain because he was in the same struggle.

Chapter 19

Uptown Philly

Crispy's mom, Manda, played the keyboard on the piano at church, praising The Lord as people shouted and danced around, feeling the Holy Ghost.

The church had almost every row full of church attenders, as they did every Sunday.

Manda raised all her kids in the church, but none of them, especially Crispy, was dry, their communication level being bad for years. She never accepted money from him, or anything, because Manda knew where the money came from.

When church ended, Manda was one of the few people left behind to clean up and get more prayers in, before heading home, which was the in projects.

"Bye, Manda, we're about to leave. Are you good?" The pastor, a tall, bald head black man asked, before leaving.

"Yes. God Bless y'all," Manda replied.

"Good night, Ms. Manda," the pastor's wife answered for the pastor because she hated Manda for many reasons. One was how she tried to always flirt with her husband.

Manda did a little more cleaning, then went to pray in the front row, and made her worship to the Lord.

While praying, she heard noises behind her, which made her look back to see two men standing behind her with pipes they found outside.

"If I was you, old bitch, I'd keep praying. You gonna need that," Twin said.

"Nah, cuz, praying ain't gonna get her outta this one," Lil Hak added, slapping the heavy metal pipe against his hand.

"What happens in the dark will always come out in the light," Manda stated.

"I like this bitch," Lil Hak said, looking at the bottle of holy water.

"This is a place of worship. What y'all hoodlums gonna do, beat me up in here?" she asked.

"No, we gonna kill you for the sake of your son," Twin said, before slapping her with his pipe, knocking Manda to the floor, and busting her head wide open.

"Ahhhhhh," she screamed, as Twin started to swing the pipe at her skull until she stopped moving.

Lil Hak poured holy water all over Manda, while Twin went to work, bashing her head into the church carpet.

Lil Hak jumped in and started beating Manda with a pipe, also. Seconds later, they saw a deacon come out from the back to see what the loud noise was. When he saw what was going on, the Deacon wished he'd never came out.

Twin pulled out his gun and shot the Deacon twice in his head, before seeing his job was done.

"Job well done." Lil Hak started walking out with Twin.

***

North Philly

Crispy's sister had called him ten minutes ago, telling him their mom was found dead at a church. He didn't even cry, nor get over emotional because his mom wasn't shit, and never had been.

"You straight, babe?" asked a red bone stripper he took home from the club.

"Go back to sleep, bitch," Crispy told her, as he tried to not think about who killed his mother. He left his room and called Sin, pacing back and forth in his living room.

"Ayo, bull," Sin answered, sounding like he was in a club.

"They killed my mom."

"What?"

"I just got the call. They found her dead in the church."

"Damn, cuz. No worries, we gonna get them niggas, bull. Calm down," Sin told him.

"I'ma kill all them niggas, I swear to Allah, bro."

"I'm with you, cuz. Tomorrow, come by the crib," Sin stated.

"I'ight, dog. Where is Dawgg?"

"Wit me in the club, bro. we are mobbing in here," Sin said.

"Ok, cool. I love you."

"Likewise, bull. Love you, fo," Sin replied.

Crispy walked back into his room to see the stripper on the king size bed, fingering herself. Crispy needed something to take his mind off his mom's death. He pulled out his dick and she jumped out of bed to suck him off. The woman sucked and slurped on his dick, going crazy. She was deep throating him with ease, working her phat lips, wrapping them around the base of his shaft, until he came in her mouth. Crispy fucked the bad bitch all night, then kicked her out.

Romell Tukes

Chapter 20

South Philly

Twin was posted in his projects with Lil Hak, who had just pulled up with six niggas on dirt bikes, chilling, enjoying the day.

"This Mandy nigga planning on sliding to New Jersey to hit up the casinos in Atlantic City. You trying to roll?" Lil Hak asked, smoking a blunt of weed.

"Hell nah. The last time we did that, I had to stab a nigga over Gee and Sosa," Twin said, thinking about when they were younger, running up in casinos.

"I'ight, fuck it then, cuz. But niggas talking about what happen to Crispy's mom," Lil Hak stated, laughing.

"That was some wild shit, but I feel bad killing her in da church. We might go to hell for that one, bro. I gotta go make Salat for that." Twin was serious, but Lil Hak laughed at him.

"Bro, I hate to tell you this, but most likely, we are both sliding into that hell fire. But I am asking for forgiveness," Lil Hak admitted.

"Nigga, how does that work? Kill a nigga, then go ask for forgiveness, and do it again?" Twin asked.

"Bro, I don't know. This street shit be having a nigga mind frame fucked up. I feel like I'm more committed to the streets than my own religion, and I be feeling like a clown." Lil Hak knew having one foot in the game and the other in Islam was the worst thing a person could do, because it would sooner or later backfire.

"What y'all niggas talking about?" Trilla said, as he pulled up on them with a thick, beautiful chick from Twin's block, known for sniffing coke and milking niggas out of their money.

"Trying to put the young bull on game," Twin said.

"Nigga, practice what you preach, bro. But I'm about to hop in this dice game." Lil Hak went to the back of Twin's projects, where a dice game was always at.

"Trilla, how you been, ock?" Twin liked Trilla. He was loyal and a true soldier.

"Same shit, running it up, watching out for these pussy ops," Trilla said.

"I heard y'all at war with the Outlaws," the woman under Trilla stated, entering their convo.

"What?" Trilla asked.

"That's what I heard," she shot back.

"Bitch, you police or something? Matter fact, get the fuck away from me." Trilla pushed her, and she walked off, popping shit.

"Shawntey crazy. That bitch killed her boyfriend back in the day," Twin told him, forgetting to tell Trilla how she be burning niggas.

"Fuck her. I'm about to slide to North Philly anyway," Trilla replied

"You seen Lez?" Twin asked.

"His phone been off for two days."

"I'ight, I'ma stop by his crib later because he owe me some money."

"You too," Trilla replied.

"That's Lez for you. But ayo, ain't Dawgg his ex-girlfriend's brother, or something?"

"Hell yeah."

"I forgot about that. Fuck him. I know what needs to be done with Dawgg, and if Foxy want some, she can be a victim," Twin said.

"Facts, bro," Trilla said, before leaving.

***

West Philly

Lez and Valeria had just got done fucking for two days straight, having make up sex. She sucked the soul out of him. Lez's dick was so sore it couldn't move. He was fucking Valeria, and had already moved her shit back into his condo.

"Hey, babe, I ordered some food," Valeria walked into the room in lingerie, looking sexy as fuck.

"Use the CashApp card."

"I already did, daddy. I'm so happy to be back. I know the bitches you was fucking ain't have no pussy like me." She crawled into bed with him to cuddle.

"I don't know. Nowadays, all y'all bitches got some good pussy," he said, seeing her face turn up.

"Whatever."

"I'm joking," Lez told her. His phone had been dead for two days because he'd lost his charger and Valeria had a different type of phone charger, which he couldn't use.

"That's the food already? I just ordered," Valeria said, getting out of bed.

"I'm getting it, baby girl. Chill." Lez got dressed and snatched his 9mm handgun from the table.

Opening the door, he saw his gang walk right inside, Sosa and Twin.

"What's good, bro? Why you ain't been picking up? We thought Crispy or Sin popped your ass or something," Sosa played around, sitting in his living room.

"I'm straight, cuz. I need a new phone charger. I can't find my shit," Lez added.

"You had to miss a lot of money," Twin said, knowing how the west side got down.

"Zels and Big Lack been holding me down," Lez said, hearing Valeria calling his name.

"Oh, you cuffin ass nigga," Twin clowned him because Lez was always talking player shit to them about how he don't be doing no cuffing.

"Y'all crazy. But I gotta take a shower and get outside," Lez told them, giving the gang the hint to leave.

"Yeah?"

"He trying to jump back in some pussy. Come on, Sosa, we out. Niggas don't respect bros before hoes no more," Twin said, taking a half of bottle of Henny from the table.

"I see that now," Sosa added.

"Oh, y'all on some bullshit," Lez said, as Valeria kept calling him, asking about the food.

"Pussy will make a nigga do strange things," Twin said while leaving.

"I see what's going on. I'll hit y'all later, cuz," Lez said, as they walked out.

***

Northeast Philly

Sosa tried to figure out why Maggie called him at midnight last night, telling him she really needed to speak with him. She requested to meet him at city hall in the back parking lot, a low key location.

With Maggie being Block's girlfriend, he felt there was something odd. But he came anyway, to see what the vibe was.

Sosa pulled up in his Mustang Supersnake, ready to cop that new Bentley Mulsanne speed with four doors soon, because he sold the Maserati.

Since his ops knew who he was now, Sosa had to switch up his flow and move differently for cautious reasons.

Maggie was leaning on her car when he arrived. Sosa got out, hoping to make this quick, because Karlee and Zarhya wanted to go out and have dinner with him in an hour.

"Maggie, what's up? You ok?" Sosa saw a stank look on her face.

"Your brother a rat," Maggie flat out stated.

"What the fuck are you talking about?"

"I can show you better than I can tell you. Watch this video I recorded yesterday." She pulled out her iPhone and pushed play on a video she took.

Sosa saw Block talking with two officers in suits. He then handed them some wires and papers.

"Bitch ass nigga." Sosa's blood was boiling because he knew all along Block had something up his sleeve, especially when he got released after getting caught with all that shit.

"I hate that hoe ass nigga. When my brother, New New, sent me the statements last week, I knew Block was vicious." She crossed her arms, sucking her teeth.

"New New? What statements?" This was all new to Sosa.

"He ratted on New New, got him 120 years. He just blew trial, thanks to Block's six statements." Maggie almost had tears in her eyes.

"Damn, Maggie, who knows about all of this shit?" Sosa asked.

"Just me, you, and New New, I guess."

"Look, let me handle this, ok. Stay calm, and don't say a word about this to nobody, Maggie," he told her in such a stern tone that she knew better than to run her mouth.

"Ok, I won't. But what are you gonna do?"

"None of your business. I am handling it, trust me," he told her.

"I believe you, Sean. But come by the club sometimes. I don't strip, but I been wanting to give you some of this for a while," she blushed.

"I'm in a relationship and I don't fuck family leftovers."

"Block was a regret and a mistake, honey," she shot back.

"Listen, I need you to act regularly, and lay low for a while, ok? Please."

"I know how the streets go, Sean." She walked off, stunting her phat ass, giving him something to look at.

"I knew it," Sosa said to himself, thinking about the encounter he had with Block, and how funny he was moving, asking dumb shit. Sosa had to re-up in a few days, so he had a small plan so take care of this issue. But the only thing was Sosa didn't know how much Block told the police, and his plan could backfire.

Romell Tukes

Chapter 21

North Philly

Sosa waited on Block in the back of a park, connected to a small lake. He came out there a few times with the gang to run trains on bitches.

Since Maggie showed him the video yesterday, Sosa couldn't sleep. One thing he hated more than a snake was a rat, family or not.

Following the code of the street was rule number one for the gang, and Sosa stood on that honor code.

Headlights from a BMW pulled up next to his car and Block hopped out swagged in a designer sweat suit. Block had been spending a lot of time in little towns on the outskirts, getting to a big bag.

"What's good, bro?" Block said.

"I'm cool, just trying to stay focused. What have you been up to?"

"Getting money, same old shit, bro."

"You recently got locked up, or some shit?" Sosa asked.

"Who told you that?"

"Just asked. I thought I heard you were in jail, but that must have been a rumor." Sosa watched his facial expression.

"That was a lie," Block got highly hype.

"Ok. Calm down."

"You heard anything else?" Block asked.

"Nah, why you ask?" Sosa saw the fear of God in his eyes.

"Just trying to make sure."

Sosa pulled out a gun. He was sick of Block talking.

"What the fuck?" Block couldn't believe what was taking place.

"You a dirty nigga," Sosa told him, putting the gun to his head.

"Sean, I don't know what's going on, but I love you, bro." Block's eyes got glossy.

"Nigga, you was talking to police and ratted on New New. Let me ask you this, how long you been snitching?"

Block waited before answering the question because he knew Sean's gun game was serious and on point.

"I fucked up, young bull," Block told him, knowing his little brother deserved the truth.

"What did you do?"

"I snitched to the DEA. They trying to build a case on you and daddy."

"You ratted on your own blood, huh? You a real bitch." Sosa couldn't believe how low he would stoop in hard times.

"I'm sorry. They tried to give me a life sentence for some shit. What you want me to do, bro?" Block protested.

"Nigga, you play gangsta."

"They don't have a lot on you, though. I promise."

"The last time you saw them, they made you wear a wire?"

"Yeah, but you didn't say anything to railroad yourself."

"Thank you, I guess," Sosa laughed.

"You my little brother, Sean. We're bigger than this," Bock said, trying to size Sosa up to take his gun.

Sosa saw the look in Block's eyes, as if he wanted to bust a move, so he did it for him.

Boc. Boc. Boc. Boc. Boc. Boc.

Block fell into the lake, just as Sosa figured he would.

Sosa walked to his car, throwing the murder weapon into the trash, and getting into his car, pulling off.

On the drive home, Sosa saw a car tailing him, so he played a little game and drove to Southwest on Bartram, then busted a quick U-turn to get a good look into the SUV, but the tints were too dark.

Sosa sped up, getting behind the SUV's bumper and flashing his lights until the truck pulled over.

When he got out and went to the SUV, he pulled his gun out, walking slowly, like a cop pulling someone over.

The driver rolled his window down, and when Sosa saw who it was, he couldn't believe it.

"Dad?"

"Get inside," Barry told him smoothly, before rolling up his window.

"I was wondering who'd been following me, pops," Sosa said, as Barry turned down the old school jams.

"Shut up and listen. Your brother was trying to throw us under the bus to save his own ass. A good friend of mine, well a cop on my payroll, locked Block up, and he dropped a few dimes. The case made it to the DEA, that's our only real worry as of now. I saw what you did in the park."

"What are you thinking about?" Sosa said, hearing Barry laugh because he knew more than his son knew.

"I like you, Sosa."

Hearing his dad call him by his street name made him think of how much more Barry knew about him.

"So, you knew this whole time who I was?" Sosa asked, as his dad drove towards Uptown.

"Yep, but you delineate a good cover up. Block was too blind to see, but I'm old school. You did right with Block. We don't condone rats or snakes in this family. Block had a real bad egomaniacal mind frame. That was his downfall. But now you're about to take his spot in the family," Barry said, pulling up to Sosa's crib.

"Me?"

"No, you, son. I need you, and now you're the plug," Barry told him.

"Damn, pops, this big."

"It's gonna be facile and smooth, but understand, you're about to elaborate on a new level in the game," Barry explained.

"Thanks, pops. I know the enchiridion and glue to these streets, so have no worries," Sosa told him.

"The night you came to me, wanting to sell drugs, I saw it in your eyes. You were hungry to feed the people around you, and I respect that." Barry always respected a man who put his friends on because it said a lot about his character.

"I'ma finish what Block could not complete."

"Tomorrow, I want you to come by my crib so I can give you something."

"I'ight bet."

"One last thing, son." Barry stopped Sosa as he was about to get out of the car.

"Yeah?"

111

"If you cross me, I'll kill you myself. Good night. Love you," Barry said, pulling off.

Sosa knew his dad meant every word of what he said, but Sosa wondered how Barry knew where he lived.

He left his car across town, but it was cool, he figured. Sosa want to take a hot shower and get out of his murder clothes, hoping the shit he'd done tonight wouldn't backfire.

***

West Philly

Kilow drove down a dangerous block, known for its heavy drug trafficking and violence, thanks to the Outlaws.

He saw a nigga named Rae, who had just come home from prison on the block, selling. He was an Outlaws member, but very few knew he was a block tipper, which was a low key rat that snitched on other dealers to get them off the block so they could make more money.

Kilow smiled and pulled his car to the curb, flashing his sirens, as two fiends both ran off. But Rae saw Kilow get out and didn't move, hoping Kilow wasn't on his bullshit.

"My man, Rae, welcome home."

"Thanks, Kilow."

"They didn't rape you in the big house for that rape charge?" Kilow asked.

"Come on, Kilow. I ain't know she was 16, bro. She had a fake ID," Rae explained himself for his recent rape charge that he'd just done three years for.

"That's what they all say, fam. But look, I need to know about a girl named Eva being killed by your people."

"I never heard of her, Kilow. So much shit going on, I don't know right from left," Rae said, seeing niggas from across the street watch his moves.

"Ok, bet," Kilow said, while grabbing Rae by his collar and tossing him on the hood of his car.

"Man, this police brutality," Rae screamed.

"Shut up, rapist," Kilow said, searching him to find drugs in his back pocket.

"That's not mines, Kilow. Somebody put that there, bro," Rae said, before Kilow cuffed him up and threw him in the back of his undercover car.

"Kilow, don't take me downtown, please," Rae cried.

"Tell me something. Do you know who is causing all this mayhem out here? Talk." Kilow hit the jackpot.

"A nigga name Sosa. I heard he like a ghost, bro. But dangerous. There is a cat named Lez from around this way, he has been dropping bodies down here for a while," Rae said, as Kilow pulled into a complex building.

"Tell me more about his Lez," Kilow said, parking his work car, looking around.

"He killed two of my cousins," Rae said, as Kilow took him inside the building.

"What else?" Kilow walked Rae upstairs to the rooftop and listened to him talk.

"Where are we going?" Rae said, while Kilow pushed him towards the edge. Then he took the cuffs off of Rae and kicked him off the roof. Kilow called it in as a suicide and walked downstairs.

***

South Philly

Twin and Zels walked in Twin's crib to see the bad bitches drinking and listening to music.

"What the fuck is this?" Twin asked Traina, who rolled her eyes at him, and focused on Zels.

"Hey, Zels," said Traina, turning down the music from the living room stereo.

"What's up with y'all?" Zels saw how good Traina and her girls were looking.

113

"I'm going to handle something in the back, cuz. I'll be right back, then we go out to Delaware," 'Twin said, making his way to his room to put some money up.

"Zels, are you single?" ReRe asked, a tall, thick redbone, with a fake ass that needed a lift.

"It depends on who is asking," he replied, looking at Traina eying him.

"Me and Igga," ReRe said smiling. She always thought he was handsome, and his name was going crazy in the city.

"No disrespect, but the woman I would even give a second of my time to is Traina," he said, as Traina coughed.

"Oh, we ain't know. Maybe, girl, you should have said that was your low key boo," Igga said, giving Traina an evil eye because she told them he was single.

"This is new to me," Traina said.

"I'm waiting on your move," Zels stated, seeing Traina freeze up and get nervous.

Twin came back out and saw all the awkward looks.

"Y'all good?" Twin asked.

"Yeah, bull, we out. Holla at me, Traina," Zels said, walking out with Twin.

Chapter 22

Uptown Philly

Sosa's dad gave him a note with an address on it and a time. He drove to the location early in the morning, while it was still all dark outside.

Now that he was in position, Sosa wanted to expand. Luckily, Lil Hak had family in New Jersey. Lez had people in Delaware, trying to get some paper, so Sosa had a few small ideas to let his nuts hang.

The address on the paper was right in front of him, as Sosa parked the car, looking at the Hala store.

"What he fuck is that shit?" Sosa asked himself, looking around, hoping it wasn't a set up because he didn't know who to trust.

Pulling the key out of his pocket, he walked into a small Hala shop, looking around for the surprise his dad said was somewhere inside the shop.

Walking around, he saw nothing. Then, when Sosa turned around, there was a door leading to somewhere. Not wasting time, he opened it.

Back the door was a cold freezer and a butcher shop, with all types of animals hanging upside down, waiting to be slaughtered.

Sosa saw a stack of something that looked like meat piled up in the corner. But when he got closer, Sosa couldn't believe his eyes. It was bricks.

"Damn, it's litty," Sosa started transferring the bricks to his car, back and forth, which became a real exercise type morning for him.

He called up Lil Hak and Lez, who were both sleeping until he woke them up, to help divide up everything and tell them his new position. They were happy knowing it was time to get richer.

***

Green County Prison, PA

Gee finally left the box and was sent back to his unit, since Tatted Mike took the body they caught. One of the Outlaw niggas died in the coma, and somebody had to take the jailhouse body. Luckily, Tatted Mike did.

The prison shipped Tatted Mike to the death row section of the jail, where he would await pre-trail for the first degree murder Gee really caught.

Gee had just got back to his cell. He was putting his stuff up inside the locker, mostly commissary he had before going to the box.

"Ayo, Gee," someone yelled his name down the tier. Gee peeped out to see Josh and Bee there, happy to see him.

"Y'all going to the yard?" Gee asked.

"Yeah, come out," Josh replied.

Gee grabbed his ID and left the cell to go talk with the gang outside for a whole rec yard.

On the way outside, a few of Gee's homies stopped him and showed him love for what he did. Problem and the rest of the crew were sent to the other side of the prison.

"We missed you, bro," Bee said, hugging Gee.

"Facts, I really was back there stressing, cuz" Gee told them, stepping into the yard.

"I heard Tatted Mike took that body for y'all?" Josh asked, walking the yard track inmates ran on.

"Yeah, they was trying to pin that shit on me, but Tatted Mike took it. I got so much love and respect for him," Gee said from his heart because Tatted Mike could've played dumb and let Gee fuck up his time.

"What's the move on them niggas, bro? We been waiting on you to make the call, cuz," Bee said.

We did what we had to already. So, tell everybody to fall back. As long as these fools play cool, we play cool," Gee said.

"Max told niggas he ain't want no smoke, and we were just waiting on the green light," Josh stated.

"It's cool, young bull," Gee said nodding his head to a few Pittsburg niggas posted up on the wall, talking.

"A'ight, cool, but you lost mad weight back there." Bee looked at how frail his boy got in the box.

"I'ma get it back," Gee confirmed.

"Shit, I don't know. I got out of SHU last year and I haven't done a push up since, bro. Real talk," Josh told Gee, who used to work out hard on weights.

"That's why I don't be on no fucking body building shit because when you lose that shit, it's over," Bee stated.

"True," Josh added.

"The gang is doing good out there," Gee said.

"I heard." Bee's cousins always filled him in on what was going on.

"Lez turned up." Josh had been cool with Lez since kids.

"All of them," Gee added.

"Facts, I can't wait until I get out there to get a bag," Bee said, as all of them agreed.

***

Chester Philly

On the outskirts of Philly was the city of Chester, where Sin's baby mother Bianca worked at.

Bianca had been at the H&M clothing store for a long time now, and she'd become the manager there last year. In a few minutes, her shift would be over, and she could go home to her baby girl and son.

Having a baby daddy like Sin was a blessing and a curse because financially, he was there, but being a good dad wasn't his best trait.

She cleaned up around the store and texted her new boo thang until it was time to go home.

Bianca eventually locked up the store and walked to her truck on the phone, laughing and joking.

"Your name Bianca?" Lil Hak popped up out of the cut, looking her up and down.

"Yes, I am. But who are you?"

"Jason."

"Ok. I'm Freddy." She sucked her teeth and walked off.

Lil Hak cocked his gun and she turned around to see a pistol to her face.

"Where can I find Sin?"

"Home in Darby." She got nervous and went into shock, having a seizure.

"Thank you," Lil Hak said, pulling the trigger to shoot her in the head.

Lil Hak walked off, thinking how smart Sin was for living in an upper class area.

***

Downtown Philly

Sosa, Karlee, and Zarhya all went out for drinks at an after work spot, where lawyers, doctors, and cops came when they got off shift.

"How many drinks did you have?" Sosa asked Zarhya, seeing her gulp glass after glass.

"Not enough. I don't got school tomorrow and you're not my dad," Zarhya giggled

"Whatever. But how's school?" Sosa asked Zarhya because, since Block's funeral this morning, she had been acting strange.

"Great, I've been passing everything with flying colors," Zarhya said.

"We've been studying with each other," Karlee said.

"That's good. Y'all two got the same classes?" Sosa asked.

"Nah, but I took her classes years ago, so I know some things," Karlee stated.

"She's really smart. You got a winner," Zarhya told him. She really liked Karlee.

"I know."

118

"Don't fuck up," Karlee threatened him jokingly, as Sosa ordered more drinks.

"I miss Block," Zarhya said sadly, drinking to her brother's death.

When they found Block's body in the lake, she cried all day and wanted to know why.

"Me too, but Allah got him now," Sosa told her, seeing an evil eye.

"Why do people keep killing people?" Zarhya said. Another round of drinks came, and she snatched two, gulping them back to back.

Even Karlee looked at Zarhya, knowing she was going hard on the liquor. But she knew the loss of their brother emotionally crushed her.

"Zarhya let me ask you something," Sosa's voice got serious.

"Yes?"

"If I die, you gonna drink yourself to death instead of being strong?" Sosa asked her, watching her put down the drink.

"Why would you even say some shit like that, Sean?" Zarhya said, feeling like throwing up because she'd had too many drinks.

"Look at you."

"But you and daddy all I got left. You know what's up with mommy," Zarhya tried to talk in code, but he'd already told Karlee about his mom's mental sickness.

"We all want you to be strong because you are the family back-bone," Sosa told her.

"But I—" Zarhya was about to vomit all over the table, but jumped up and ran to the restroom.

"I am going to help her." Karlee got up.

"Thanks."

"Go easy on her, Sean. She's grieving, unlike you, for some reason." Karlee walked off, not seeing one bit of sorrow in his face all day.

"Only if you knew," Sosa whispered, pulling out his phone to call Twin, who had texted him early this morning in code, saying

Dawgg almost took him out. Sosa was sick of all this drama, especially with so much money flowing in.

***

South Philly

Twin and Zels posted up in front of the Wilson Projects, trying to come up with a plan to get back at Dawgg.

"Weezy F and Baggs out the hospital yet?" Twin said, hanging up his phone call.

"I think so, young bull. I'ma called to check," Zels said as his new diamond chains sparkled in the dark.

"Call later, we need to figure this shit out. Them clowns almost caught me slippin' coming out that corner on 19th and Sigel," Twin said.

"Luckily Weezy F and Baggs popped out to save the day," Zels said as Trilla came out of one of the buildings.

Zels and Trilla didn't really have a relationship because of some childhood beefs when they were twelve years old.

"What's up?" Trilla asked.

"Plotting," said Twin.

"I heard what happened. You good?"

"Nigga, I'm still here, so I'm great," Twin shot back with an attitude.

"I'ight, just asking. I'm about to slide out to West Philly, cuz," Trilla told Twin, walking right past Zels with a light smirk.

"That nigga a goofy," Zels said, as Twin paced back and forth, thinking about what happened. He texted Sosa, but the reply was short because Sosa had to take Zarhya to his crib, she was so drunk.

"Ayo, I got a plan, bro," Twin said, smiling like an evil kid.

"What?'

"Are you using your bike?"

"Nah, why you ask?" Zels saw a weird look on Twin's face and knew he was up to something

Sosa Gang

***

South Philly

On 2nd and Dickerson, it looked like a block party. Everybody was out, women, kids, hustlers, killers, and Dawgg, with his crew, standing in front of a row house.

"Damn, Dawgg, since you moved out here, you are acting brand new," Shierka said, wearing barely nothing, except jail shorts and a tank top in Air Max 95, looking curvy and sexy.

"Shierka, we went to school together. I can never change on your sexy ass," Dawgg replied pouring a bottle of lean in a cup.

"Ok." Shierka replied, as her girls were fucking with Dawgg's friends. Shierka was Gee's sister, from the Sosa Gang. But she fucked with the rest of the gang.

"You smoking?" Dawgg asked Shierka, who drove his new smoke gray Benz-G Wagon truck that he'd copped yesterday.

Sin met with Dawgg two days ago for his re-up and heard about the murder of Bianca. Now he had to be a single parent. Sin was on fire; he didn't even look like the old Sin. He'd turned into a mad man overnight.

Dawgg saw an unfamiliar motorcycle, pulling down the block. But bikes were regular in the city, especially in South Philly. As the bike got closer, Dawgg saw Twin's face. But before Dawgg could yell, shit went left.

Tat. Tat. Tat. Tat. Tat. Tat. Tat. Tat. Tat. Tat. Tat.

Bullets tore Shierka's breasts, and Dawgg got hit several times, before Twin sped off on the bike, leaving the dead.

Romell Tukes

Chapter 23

Sharon Hill, Philly

Barry grabbed Elina's phat ass cheeks as she moaned and dug her fingers into his flesh, as he went deeper.

"Ohhh yesss. Fuck me," she screamed. Barry's balls banged against her butt, as she reached a shattering orgasm.

Elina's muscles in her pussy constricted around his pole, as he went in and out in slow, then fast motion.

"You want me?" he asked, feeling his build up.

"Yesss, babyyyy," she begged as he stroked his rod deeper into her sex box. Barry pounded into Elina harder than ever.

Her body squirmed beneath his, and then she wrapped her legs around his waist, as he finally came inside of Elina.

She wanted to ride, so Elina flipped and got on top, slowly climbing on the dick. She began riding him at top speed. She bounced up and down on his rigid pole, while he played with her breasts.

Barry squeezed the jiggling mound of flesh and pinched the erect nipples.

"Uhhmmmm," she moaned as her ass rose and fell onto his dick.

Her ass slapped against his thighs with each downward movement. Then she stopped, lowering herself to his cock.

She started sucking him off, going crazy, making his toes curl up.

"Shit, girl, you trying to give me a heart attack, he said, as she swallowed him like a true freak, until he came again. Elina took a shower because she had to go to work as a paralegal.

***

North Philly

Crispy arrived at a local car wash to meet with Sin, who was on his way to talk about what happened last night to Dawgg, when the news hit him, early this morning.

A Dodge Demon pulled up and Sin was behind the wheel, blasting rap music.

The look on Sin's face said it all. First his baby mother, then Dawgg. He knew something had to give soon because they were taking big losses.

"You heard what they did to the young bull last night?" he asked Crispy, pulling out a cig to smoke.

"Yeah, cuz, I heard it was Twin on the bike shooting."

"Go figure."

"This shit getting crazy. Them clowns killed my mom in a church, cuz," Crispy stated, still hurt about that event.

"I had to bury my BM, bro, so I know how you feel. The main little nigga is that Sosa kid. I can't get ahold of this little nigga because from the looks of things, he's calling the shots," Sin told him in deep thought, watching the busy streets, just in case something popped off.

"You sure it's him? What about Twin or Lez?" Crispy asked, not trying exclude them two deadly niggas.

"Nah, trust me. He moves like a boss."

"What do we do now?"

"I'ma put something together, but the plug talking about he see a drop in the payments, and how much we copping," said Sin.

"All this shit distracting us, cause them niggas starting to take over all the Philly blocks. Even the D.C. crew having trouble eating out here." Crispy had been paying close attention to the money flow from each crew in the city, and Sosa Gang been eating.

"That little nigga smart."

"What do you mean?"

"He's killing people off our blocks to take them over to move product." Sin never could figure it out, until now.

"You think he's that smart?" Crispy asked.

"Fuck what we think, look what's happening, cuz. Them niggas took four of our blocks in two months."

124

"Facts."

"I need to find out who is supplying them," Sin thought out loud.

"We know it's not Block," Crispy stated, after hearing about how they found the city's biggest plug in a lake, dead.

"Block wouldn't fuck with them anyway. He was big time. These clowns on a come up."

"So maybe they killed him?" Crispy asked, trying to add up everything Sin was saying.

"Nah, they ain't that crazy, bro." Sin thought Crispy was on to something, but he was trying to figure out how they were locking down the city. Somebody had to be helping them.

***

Sosa was on his way to pick up Karlee from college to take her out to eat. Driving through North Philly, he was in his Mustang, listening to Tee Grizzly's album, trying to put another plan together to get richer, but with out of town money.

The kilo's he got from Barry's Hala shop was a gift. Barry told him but the next wave was on him, cash on deck.

Sosa stopped at a light. He looked to his left for a quick second and saw Sin and Crispy having a conversation.

"Got'cha now." Sosa reached under the seat, while creeping into the car wash lot and rolling down his window.

Sosa knew if he hopped out on them, he would most likely get hit, or worse, killed, because he saw their guns poking out of their shirts.

Pulling up on them, Crispy happened to look first and duck.

Boc. Boc. Boc. Boc. Boc. Boc.

Sin got hit once before Crispy started busting back at the Mustang, which was racing away from the scene.

Crispy rushed to help Sin, who got hit in his arm, but was ok, besides blood and pain.

"I'm taking you to my cousin's crib. She is a nurse," Crispy helped him into his car, taking him to South Philly.

***

South Philly

Twin hide out a little bitch crib name Kianay until shit coded down with the Dawgg killing because word was out that Twin did the drive by.

"You hungry baby?" Kianay said coming out the back room smoking a blunt in lingerie looking curt tatted up.

"Nah, you can't cook anyway," Twin told her while watching his favorite TV show, Power.

"I can try," she jumped in his lap, looking at the two handguns on the table.

"Order something."

"Ok, I will, babe, but I got a question."

"What?" Twin hated it when she talked because Kianay always asked some dumb shit.

"Did you really kill Dawgg?" Kianay knew all the hood info. Her ears stayed to the street.

"Who told you that shit?" Twin quizzed.

"I forget where I heard it but I did."

"Well, I ain't killed nobody, ok. Go to the liquor store and pick up some food," he told her.

"You know you can trust me right?" She said, as he laughed in her face.

"Didn't you tell on your baby's father?"

"He was beating on me, Twin."

"So, you send him to jail, instead of walking away?" Twin asked, not down with niggas hitting on women, but he didn't like people sending someone to jail. He believed in holding courts in the streets.

"If you was a female and a nigga beat your ass, what would you do?" She started to get upset.

Just as Twin was going to respond a cop pulled up on them with his head out the window staring at them. "What the fuck you want, pig?" spat Twin.

"Your gang, the top dawgs, because if we don't get y'all, then the Outlaws will kill them all," the cop laughed.

"So I give you a name, I go free?" Trilla asked, sounding interested.

"No, I'ma need names, victims, and you to take the stand at trial and write a few statements." The cop saw Trilla in deep thought.

"Ok, but when will I be able to leave?" Trilla asked the black cop he used to see all the time harassing niggas in the hood.

"Yep."

"Ok, you know the kid, Dawgg?" Trilla asked.

"Yeah, someone killed him and a young woman a few days ago."

"Yes. I know who did it because he came back and told me."

"Who?"

"Twin, from the Sosa Gang, killed them on a bike," Trilla ratted, knowing the cop would buy his story, even though it was true.

"This shit is good. I'll be back in with a statement, and write everything you just told me down, ok." The cop rushed off.

"Ayo, Kilow, I'm gonna be safe out there after I do this?" Trilla asked the cop, who was Kilow, the dirtiest cop in Philly at the moment.

"People snitch everyday out here. It's a part of the game, young bull."

"They are dangerous, especially Lez and Sosa," Trilla stated, as Kilow turned around.

"All I need you to do is tell me what you know, then keep your fucking mouth shut," Kilow said.

"As long as I'm free, I'll do whatever," Trilla stated.

"I bet." Kilow walked off.

***

Downtown Philly, Hours Later

Philly International Airport parking lot was dark out in the far back, but you could see the stars in the sky as airplanes took off. Kilow saw Lez arrive in a blue Range Rover with tints. He'd called him to talk about Trilla's name dropping season earlier.

Kilow couldn't keep covering Lez's ass, especially with the DEA and his boss on his ass because no arrest were being made.

"What's up?" Lez got out of the truck with a diamond chain and Rolex watch. He was on his way out to a club with the whole gang.

"We got a problem again. It seems to me y'all letting the wrong people in y'all circle."

"What the fuck you mean?" Lez screwed up his face.

"You know Trilla?" Kilow said, passing Lez the statements Trilla wrote.

"I know the young bull. What's this?" Lez read the paper and Trilla was telling on the whole gang about bodies, drugs, and much more shit that Lez didn't even know about.

"Take care of it. I'm not," Kilow turned to walk off.

"Aye, can you find me Sin and Crispy? They had something to do with Eva death." Lez saw Kilow's muscles in his face tighten.

"I'ight, but you need to watch yourself."

"Ok thanks, bro," Lez replied

"I ain't do it for you," Kilow said, before getting in his car, driving off.

Chapter 24

Green County Prison, PA

Gee got done reading the letter about his sister's death and he couldn't believe it. The last time they talked was the same day she got killed, from what the letter said.

Sitting in his cell, all he could do was reflect on her. That was the bad thing about prison. When something bad happened, it would weigh a person down because you had all the time in the world to think.

"Bitch ass niggas," Gee said, thinking out loud, knowing that was Dawgg who got killed too.

Gee knew Dawgg was down with the Outlaws. When he found out Dawgg got killed also, something didn't make sense. But right now, all he could do was grieve over Shierka, and pull himself together while in jail to conceal the weakness of showing any type of emotion.

Gee placed the letter under his thin mattress and laid down, thinking about how crazy life was out there.

Losing people close made Gee feel like it was all he fault because if he was home, they would still be alive, in his head. Gee promised himself that when he got out, he would find his sister's killer and leave the streets alone.

**

West Philly

Foxy arrived at her brother's funeral with her beautiful mom, who was still hurt over the death of her son. When Foxy got the news, she was at a friend's house. The tears hadn't stopped since the terrible news.

Looking around the graveyard as the funeral was about to begin, she saw a bunch of young men arriving on four wheelers and dirt bikes, showing love and respect to Dawgg.

"They killed my baby boy," Foxy's mom cried, sitting down, looking into the sky, and crying behind her dark shades.

"It's ok, mom. You got time. I'm still here," Foxy told her beautiful mom, wondering who killed her brother.

"I love you, Foxy. You all I have left."

"I'm not going nowhere, mom. I swear," Foxy said, seeing Crispy and Sin show up with forty goons playing the background.

Foxy only knew a few of Dawgg's friends, but she hoped they would ride for the death of her brother, like real friends should.

The ceremony started and everybody got a quiet, looking at her brother in the black casket. It was killing her, just sitting in the front row.

Foxy wiped the tears off her face, trying to be the soldier she truly was, but it was easier said than done.

***

Philly International Airport, Philly

Sosa, Zels, Twin, Lez, Trilla, and Lil Hak all took a first class flight on their way to Atlanta, so they could get away from the city for a few days.

"I never been to da A, cuz," Zels told Sosa, sitting behind him on the flight.

"It's gonna be litty in the club. This nigga, Lil Durk, supposed to be in Blue Flame with that New York nigga, Lil Tjay, so I know we gonna have fun," Sosa said, thinking if he should visit his mom, who was at a metal hospital in Atlanta.

The relationship between him and his mom was nothing because she didn't even remember who he was, due to her mental sickness.

"Go to sleep," Lil Hak told them, sitting next to Lez, trying to sleep.

"Nigga, we on our way to ATL. Fuck sleeping, it's turn up time, young bull," said Twin, thinking of how he was going to Peachtree to go shopping.

"Don't be down here tricking all your bread, Trilla," Sosa said, seeing Trilla was acting differently and distant.

"Nah, I'm just chilling," Trilla replied.

"How many days are we out here?" Lez asked everybody.

"The weekend," Twin said.

"Y'all think Big Lack finna be good at holding shit down until we touch?" Lez asked.

"Big Lack smart, he know what to do and what not to do" Lil Hak added.

"Facts." Zels had known Big Lack for a longtime.

"Twin, you heard who won that Lakers game?" Lez asked.

"Nah," Twin said, knowing Lez was still a little mad at him for killing his ex-girlfriend's brother.

"We should be landing in two hours. I got us a limousine," Sosa added.

"I'ight," Zels got hyped.

"It's about to be a movie out here," Lil Hak said.

***

Atlanta, GA

Later that night, the club had a VIP section in the back, filled with sexy dancers, shaking ass and popping their pussy for them bands.

"You gonna take care of what we talked about tonight?" Sosa asked Lil Hak, who was near him, getting a lap dance.

"You know I am," Lil Hak replied.

"Lez came thru for us. I'm glad he got someone on the inside now," Sosa said drinking.

"Facts," Lil Hak looked at Lez and Trilla on the stage turned up, tossing bands.

"Y'all niggas whispering with strippers on the spot. What type of time y'all on?" Zels said, joking with them to get dirty looks.

"Shut up," Sosa said, calling a bottle girl to order more bottles, as a big booty girl approached him with a G-String on. But Sosa could smell her strong odor, and so could Lil Hak.

"Damn. That you smelling like that?" Lil Hak asked the woman, who smelled herself, embarrassed.

"I'm going to freshen up. I was dancing all night," she said, leaving.

Lil Hak saw Trilla heading outside and got up. Lil Hak followed Trilla through the crowds. Trilla was rushing to the parking lot, with his phone in hand.

Lil Hak knew Trilla was up to something, but he couldn't put his finger on it, until Lez told him and Sosa that Trilla had been working with the cops.

Once Trilla had his back turned to him on the phone, Lil Hak made his move, pulling out his weapon.

"Get the fuck off the phone, snitch ass nigga," Lil Hak told him, as Trilla slowly lowered the phone.

"Hak, what up, bull?"

"Nigga, who you work for?" Lil Hak asked.

"Kilow, bro, but it's bigger than him. The DEA is-"

Boc. Boc. Boc. Boc.

Lil Hak blew Trilla's brains out, splattering blood all over a red Lambo that was parked right there.

"Rat ass nigga." Lil Hak saw the block was empty and nobody heard the gunshots, so he made his way back into the club, after tossing the gun in a dumpster.

Lil Hak got a text from his boy, Gyso, saying Big Lack just got killed, and Lil Hak's heart dropped. He rushed into the club, as the security guards looked out the door because they thought someone let off a firecracker outside. But regardless, they weren't going out there to find out.

Inside the VIP, everybody was there with a group of dancers.

"They killed Big Lack," Lil Hak told everybody.

"What? I just spoke to him two hours ago," Lez said pulling out his phone, and pushing the dancer off his lap to call Big Lack. He got no reply. Then he received a few calls from niggas, saying Big Lack got murdered.

Romell Tukes

Chapter 25

Green County Prison, PA

Gee had been fucked up for the past two weeks, since hearing about his sister's death.

He used to always tell Shierka to stay out of the hood, and if she was going to hang out, then hang out on the outskirts of Philly.

Her not listening lead to her death, and he felt like it really was his fault because he was supposed to be out there.

His mom went to the wake last night for the funeral in two days. There was a big delay on the funeral because the church where his mom wanted to have the funeral hard to book, but he knew this was part of the game.

Gee didn't call any of his boys out there because he wasn't ready to speak to anybody, except his mom.

Being locked in his cell was all he wanted to do. But there was so much bullshit going on in the jail, he couldn't even keep a low profile.

Three more Sosa Gang niggas pulled up this week, all from his hood. It was time to go to lunch, so Gee came out of the cell, fully dressed in his prison uniform, ready to walk to the chow hall.

"Ayo, Gee," a young bull named Strip yelled out, walking towards him on the tier.

"Strip, what's up, cuz?"

"I gotta put a bug in your ear, cuz," Strip said.

"A what, nigga?"

"I have to tell you something," Strip said nervously.

"You should have said that," Gee hated when people made shit harder than it was already.

"These niggas, Bea and Josh, about crack them Outlaw niggas on the walk to the chow hall," Strip said.

"What? Where are they at?" Gee asked, knowing how nasty shit could get, if he didn't step on his young bulls.

"On their way to the chow hall. They said one of them Outlaw niggas killed Bee's little sister, a few years ago," Strip told him.

"Let's go," Gee left the tier, hoping to run into the men to stop the young bull, Bee, who he knew was a live wire from the streets.

Gee hated being around a lot of Sosa Gang niggas, or niggas from his block, because they were all on bullshit.

Walking through the halls, he spotted Bee and Josh in a circle, being surrounded by eight Outlaw niggas.

Gee could see they were in a heated argument, but as he got closer, Bee looked him directly in his eyes and smiled.

Bee punched the older man in his face, knocking him out, and shit went crazy.

The Outlaw niggas jumped on Bee and Josh. Gee ran to the commotion and started beating up two of them, before a few guards started hitting them all with sticks to break up the brawl.

When Gee was in cuffs with everybody else, he didn't see Strip nowhere in sight. He ran off before Gee even got a punch off.

They all went to the box, and the guards took all the Sosa Gang members off the prison yard, just in case payback would force a riot.

***

West Philly

Foxy drove out to the projects to listen to her brother's favorite song by Lil Baby. He used to listen to the song so much that she got tired of it. But now that he was gone, she loved the song.

Now she only had a memory of Dawgg, and a few items he left behind with her.

Foxy knew what came out of being a street nigga, and that was death or prison. It was just his luck that death chose him.

She knew Dawgg wasn't an angel, and he had a lot of beef in the street, but he was a good brother and father.

Foxy knew about the beef with Outlaw niggas and Sosa Gang, but she didn't know who killed her brother.

Her ex-boyfriend, Lez, was a loyal member of Sosa Gang. The niggas were crazy and violent. She saw a bunch of shit with her own eyes, when she was dealing with Lez.

The only thing she hoped was that Lez had nothing to do with Dawgg's death, or she would hate him.

***

West Philly

Lez sat there, listening to his new girl accuse him of cheating, two months into their dating.

Lez didn't even know how Valeria got into his crib, minutes ago. She rushed in, talking about how she saw a chick post up a picture of him on social media.

He let her talk, yell, and curse, until she had enough.

The chick who posted up a pic of Lez was his fifteen year old little cousin, who he basically raised. Lez hated chicks with esteem issues.

"You nasty, nigga, got pics with other bitches," Valeria yelled. She was a sexy, brown skin chick, with a crazy body, but she only fucked with baller niggas like Meek Mill and ball players.

She saw him laughing and got mad, tossing an ashtray at him. Lez jumped up, about to choke her, but he paused.

"Get the fuck out, bitch."

"What?"

"Get out," he yelled.

"Baby, I'm sorry. I'm on my period," she said.

"Valeria, please leave." Lez opened the door for her, and she left in tears. Lez couldn't take it anymore. Then he took a nap, thinking about Crispy.

Romell Tukes

Chapter 26

Southwest Philly

Kars walked out his aunt's building to hop on his dirt bike and go meet up with a few of his homies.

Lil Hak was going around town wilding, and he was trying to stay away from him.

Killing Crispy's mom was his last straw because he hadn't been to sleep yet.

Walking to the alley, where he had his bike, he climbed on and started it up. He loved dirt bikes, just like a lot of young bulls in his crew.

Peeling off, he didn't see the all-black, tinted out Ford Focus behind him. At the drop of a dime, the car rammed into the bike, knocking Kars off the bike in the middle of the street he used to hustle on.

Kilow hopped out in regular clothes with is Glock 17 out, pointed at Kars.

"Don't be a bitch," Kilow said, placing cuffs on Kars.

Once cuffed up, Kilow threw Kars in the backseat of his undercover car.

***

Uptown Philly

Kilow parked in a vacated apartment building parking lot, while listening to an old 2 Pac album.

Kars didn't know what the fuck was going on, but he was starting to think Kilow wasn't a regular cop.

Kilow got on his walkie-talkie and said something in code, after he turned down the music.

When Kars saw the cop get out and look around the empty, dead area, chills went through his body.

"I'm giving you a way out. Tell me about this Sosa Gang and who is running it." Kilow sat Kars up on his driver side.

"I don't know who they are," Kars said, trying to play dumb.

"Oh yeah?" Kilow laughed and punched Kars in the stomach, almost making him throw up.

"Ok. Chill out, bro."

"Who runs the crew?"

"I don't know. I just go on drills with Lil Hak and the niggas on my side," Kars told the cop.

"Killing Crispy's mom was a drill? And having Trilla killed was a drill too, huh?" Kilow asked.

"Trilla was a rat."

"You are a rat now, also. What do you think they gonna say?"

"I ain't no snitch."

"You're a dead snitch now." Kilow pulled out his gun.

Boc. Boc. Boc. Boc. Boc.

Kilow called it in to his dispatch.

"A gun just fired shots at me. I fired back. Man down, man down, man down," Kilow screamed into the walkie-talkie.

***

Downtown Philly

Crispy was riding around with a bulletproof vest, a grade four, with a Tech 9 under the seat, and a Mack 11 in the trunk.

Losing his mom had him on go, ready to kill up the city and bury every Sosa Gang member.

His sister's car was in the shop, so he told her he would pick her up from work at the courthouse on 13th and Filbert.

Crispy's sister worked as a courthouse typist. She was the one in the courthouse typing the conversations between the defense and the counsel.

He pulled up across the street and waited for her to come out. He had to go out of town.

Minutes later, his sister came out. She had on a business suit with a suitcase.

She had a good career, but she didn't look down on Crispy for the way he lived because they both came from the same place, the slums.

Crossing the street, a motorcycle pulled up, and she paid it no mind. She was looking at Crispy getting out of his car. Since their mom got killed, they had been clicking tight.

"Duck," Crispy yelled, seeing the gunmen open fire on them, hitting his sister seven times in the back. Crispy got shot two times in his lower body, while peeling off, doing 70 mph.

Romell Tukes

Chapter 27

Fort Washington Philly

On the outskirts there was Phillyland, a neighborhood full of mansions, and one of them belonged to Barry.

The 23,519 square foot mansion with the wrap-around driveway was something Sosa looked forward to having real soon.

The apartments he had were cool, but he wanted something like this.

Sosa got out of his car and walked into his dad's huge mansion for their sit down.

"Dad?"

"Sosa, come to the kitchen," Barry yelled from the back area.

On Sosa's way to the back, he walked past Elina, wearing a tight Dior outfit that showed her pussy print.

Sosa was stuck for a minute, but he snapped out of it quickly, and looked into her eyes. She had a smirk on her face, knowing what he was just staring at.

"Hey, Sosa, good to see you," she said, strutting off, swaying her hips as her phat jiggly ass turned him on.

Sosa was so caught up in staring at her ass that he didn't even see his dad standing there.

"Fix your eyes, son," Barry joked.

"May bad."

"No need to apologize. You're a man that knows his limits." Barry gave Sosa a stern look so he would know that was all his.

"I feel you. But what you drinking?" Sosa saw his dad drinking a smoothie.

"This is my work-out drink, son. You gotta get on his fitness shit. It's the new thing," Barry stated.

"I'ma get into it soon."

"Hope so but let me show you something. When was the last time you spoke to your mom?" Barry asked, walking into the living room, pulling out some papers from the dresser.

Sosa took a look at the papers his dad just had and read over them.

"A divorce?"

"Yeah, that's from your mom. She sold the other house and moved to Atlanta last week. When she got the news of Block's death, she moved soon after. I'm surprised she ain't tell you," Barry said, sitting down.

"Damn, I know y'all been done and got separated, but I ain't know she moved to ATL. I ain't speak to her in a few weeks."

I thought she was in a mental institution. Sosa was confused but he played along.

"You know your mom, she'll shut down on everybody when closed in or feeling anxiety attacks."

"I hope she's taking meds," Sosa added.

"Me too, son. But did you fully think about what I asked you days ago?" Barry asked.

"Yeah, and I'm ready," Sosa said with confidence.

"You know what you're getting yourself into?"

"Yes."

"Ok. We need a house where my men can deliver, and I'll give you a house address where I want you, and only you, to drop off the money," Barry stated.

"Ok, that's fair."

"I say that just so we don't have any miscommunications" Barry said.

"I agree," Sosa added.

"Your brother was a snake. Never take his steps in life, son."

"How long have you known he was a snake?" Sosa asked.

"He's been stealing from me, doing side deals with my people in Vegas and Arizona, for some time now."

"So you let him get away with murder?" Sosa asked.

"I had to wait to replace him with you, and I recently saw you was ready."

"When?"

144

"The day you killed your brother. You could've told me about Block, but instead, you took it upon yourself to handle the situation yourself, and I respect that," Barry said.

"You knew I was going to kill my own brother, so you didn't have to," said Sosa

"Basically. I would hate to kill my own son."

"I bet. But that was pretty smooth, I'll say."

"I ain't made it to this age by being a slow young bull. You know that old rundown Butcher store over there on Price Street?" Barry asked.

"That abandoned spot across from the Ock store they sell Hala food at?" Sosa remembered the place briefly.

"Yes, that place. Go there tomorrow at 11:45 p.m. on the dot," Barry said, hearing the evening prayer was in for the Islamic religion.

"Ok, I'll be there."

"I know, son. But I have to make Salat (Prayer), hopefully my prayer will wash away all my sins."

"Inshallah." Sosa wasn't a Muslim but almost everybody he knew was, so he knew some stuff.

Romell Tukes

Chapter 28

Uptown, Philly

Prince Street was empty this morning at six a.m., a perfect time for Sosa to make his move. He saw the butcher shop right across the street from where he was parked.

The only thing he wasn't comfortable with was transporting the drugs alone. He was a boss and riding around in a car or van full of drugs was dumb.

He understood his father wanted to move a certain type of way, but Sosa also had his ways of doing business.

Getting out of the car, he looked around to make sure no funny shit was going on.

Sosa loved his dad, but he knew in the game, you couldn't trust a soul, especially family. His brother was a primary example.

Barry told him to enter the back of the boarded up shop and to get the key in the window seal, buried under a brick.

In the back, he found the brick with ease, and unlocked the back door, entering the place.

Looking around, he saw nothing. Walking deeper, he saw a freezer area and opened the latch on the large gray door.

As soon as he stepped foot inside, he saw a dead man hanging upside down.

Sosa could tell the killing was fresh because the blood on the floor was wet.

There were two black and gray duffle bags near the wall. He took the bags and rushed out. He knew his dad was trying to send him a message, and he respected that.

Sosa tossed the drugs in his car and went to see Lil Hak nearby, on standby.

***

"Tell them to take two duffle bags out the back and bring it up-stairs," Sosa said.

Lil Hak wasted no time in doing what he asked. His two soldiers got the duffle bags and rushed it up the stairs.

"What's that?" Lil Hak knew the bags looked heavy, but he wanted to know what was inside.

"Seventy keys."

"Seventeen or seventy, as in seven zero?" Lil Hak had to ask because, normally, Sosa would drop off five to ten keys daily, at the most.

"Seventy, nigga. We lit, bull." Sosa got excited.

"What are we gonna do with 70 keys, cuz?"

"Supply the bro's and the gang and lock down the city."

"What about the Outlaws?" Lil Hak asked.

"Fuck them," Sosa said, walking off and getting back in the car.

***

Southwest Philly

Lil Hak got the call from Sosa, saying to be ready, he would be coming any minute.

The past couple of days, he had been chilling, focused on getting to a bag, but the only issue with that was he ran out of drugs.

He knew Sosa called for a reason. He wouldn't call unless it was some important shit, or some money shit, like re-up time.

Minutes later, he saw Sosa pull up. Two of Lil Hak's goons were outside, just in case they had to slide somewhere for Sosa.

They had all types of weapons hidden throughout the block, everything from assault rifles to handguns.

When he saw Sosa get out, he saw a glow on his face like he'd just hit the lotto.

"What's up, cuz?" Lil Hak approached him with his chains swinging.

***

Downtown Philly

Traina and two of her friends came out to party and have a good time. She looked sexy in her dress that hugged her curves and showed a little cleavage.

She was dancing on a nigga in the club, getting nasty, twerking on his dick, going crazy as the City Girls song blared through the club.

Once the song was done, Traina ran off to her girls posted up by the bar, chilling, drinking.

"I'm ready to go, girl. My man blowing up my phone. You know that nigga get crazy and wanna start hitting a bitch," one of her girls said, checking her phone.

"You always fuck up the fun, bitch. Oh my god, I be hating you for that," Traina said, taking one last sip of her drink before leaving with her girls through the crowded club.

Outside, Traina took a deep breath because the club was so hot inside that she couldn't even breathe at all.

A Porsche truck pulled up next to the women and the door flew open.

Traina saw the man she was dancing on moments ago jump out with a handgun. He wasted no time as he started shooting.

Boc. Boc. Boc. Boc. Boc.

Crispy was the shooter. He shot all three women. He was going to continue to fire, until Zels and his crew came out of the lot, busting rounds at him.

Bloc. Bloc. Bloc. Bloc. Bloc. Bloc.

Crispy jumped in his tuck and pulled off, racing up the street. Sirens could be heard, but Zels picked up Traina and put her over his shoulder, driving her to the nearby hospital.

Romell Tukes

Chapter 29

West Philly

Lez and Big Chevposted up in the back of an apartment, where Big Chev lived and sold drugs.

The two men had been close for some time now. They were like brothers from another mother.

"Where are you from?" Lez asked, to see Big Chev drink straight out a bottle of dark liquor.

Big Chev drank a lot, it ran in his family, to the point where his grandpa and father died off of liquor.

Growing up in the hood with a house full of women, he learned how to be the man of the house. He learned the game early, how to fend for himself and survive.

Lez was the only person he could always turn to for help and guidance, and they were the same age.

They called him Big Chev because he stood like a giant, and he was a vicious gangsta.

Growing up in West Philly, he knew it was kill or be killed, so he quickly adapted to that mentality.

"Gloria took her ass to Miami to get her body done up. Mama Love outta pocket," Big Chev laughed.

"No, she didn't, bull." Lez couldn't believe it because Gloria was in her mid-forties, but she looked decent.

"She on some boss shit now." Big Chev shook his head.

"That's what's up. She deserves it." Lez knew how far she'd come and how she raised all those kids on her own.

"You right, bro," Big Chev said, seeing a text pop up on his phone.

"This shit dead out here tonight, bro," Lez stated.

"Oh shit, there was a big shootout at the club downtown with Zels and the Outlaws," Big Chev announced, reading the text message.

"Damn. I know Twin was there, if Zels was," Lez stated.

"Nah, they shot his sister," Big Chev stated.

"Damn, he is about to spazz out," Lez replied.

"Facts, bro."

"I'll call him," said Lez, dialing the number.

***

"That damn nigga's right there, cuz. Pull the car up on them," Sin told his little cousin. He rolled down the window.

When Sin drove through the slums of West Philly, he saw a nigga a little closer, and he realized it was them.

"Caught y'all bitch asses," Sin said, hanging out the window with a Tech 9 submachine gun.

Tat. Tat. Tat. Tat. Tat. Tat.

Big Chev got hit and Lez ducked the bullets. Seeing his friend drop, he took his gun and fired back at the Camaro.

Sin pulled off as bullets continued to hit the car.

"Chev, you good?" Lez said, seeing his boy still breathing.

"Hospital," he said in a low voice.

Lez helped him up into his GMC truck, taking him to Temple Hospital.

***

Temple Hospital, Philly

Twin waited in the Emergency waiting room with a few family members, glad the doctors just informed them Traina would make it, but her friends didn't.

When Twin got the call, he ran to the hospital because he was already nearby.

Zels called him and explained the story to him, and he really appreciated his courage.

Listening to his family talk, he almost did not even see Big Chev come to the hospital in pain, yelling.

"Oh shit, bull," Twin said, seeing Lez pushing Big Chev in on a wheelchair.

The nurses rushed out to his aid and helped him inside.

"These niggas wilding out" Lez said seriously, pacing.

"What happened?"

"Sin ran up on us," Lez said, pissed off.

"We're gonna get him," Twin said.

"What happened to Sosa?" Lez asked.

"I don't know."

"I'ma find out," Lez said, walking out of the hospital, leaving Big Chev in there before the police came.

Romell Tukes

Chapter 30

South Philly

Crispy drove through his hood early morning to pick up his car from the shop since its wheel line segment was fucked up.

He used one of his boys' trucks to move around, instead of his Benz.

Later on, Crispy had a meeting with Sin to discuss the issue, which was causing him to lose a lot of friends and family.

Crispy rode around on demon time, with a big gun on his lap, ready to smoke an opp.

The recent club shooting was the talk of the town. He knew it was go hard or die, now. But his main target was none other than Twin, his rival.

Pulling into a car dealership, Crispy had a quick reflection on his sad life and how he was raised, which led him into the streets.

Growing up, his parents were both crackheads, so he was raised bouncing home to home in foster homes and group homes.

As a young teenager, he was raped by his uncle, more than once, which made him try to commit suicide two times.

He never told nobody about being raped. It was his little secret. But at times, he felt like he needed to let it out. A few years back, he killed his uncle on the block, coming out of a dope house he was running.

Killing his uncle did not help him feel any better, as he thought he would.

Crispy needed to get at his crew for the next re-up, and to make sure they were all on point. He knew firsthand Sosa Gang wasn't the type of crew one should sleep on.

While calling his crew, his baby mother called to argue about money for their son. Even though they were not together, he still took good care of his creation.

After Crispy checked on his car, which wasn't done yet, he then went to his baby mother's crib, and ended up getting a quickie.

***

Temple Hospital

Traina was still laid up in the hospital, thinking about what happened a few days ago. She lost two of her closest friends that night, and seeing other people get shot did something to her brain.

Laying in the hospital bed, she wanted to cry so bad, but the South Philly in her wouldn't let her.

Every time she closed her eyes, she saw gun fire. She was just glad to be alive and breathing.

The knock at the door made her jump, as if it was a gun sound.

Twin and the dude who saved her life entered the room with balloons and flowers.

She looked a hot mess, hair frizzy, and her lips were chapped also.

"Damn, sister, they changed your shit bag?" Twin joked, being funny, but she is wanting to laugh at that point.

"Nigga, shut up. Thanks for coming." She looked over him to Zels standing there and smiled. He looked cute, and she owed him her life.

"You gonna smile at my little man, or say something?" Twin asked.

"What?" she said.

"I'm glad you're ok," Zels finally spoke up.

"Thanks to you for saving me," she said seriously.

"No problem. I knew who you was, so I had to."

"Well thanks," she restated.

"I have to go back. I'm keeping Zels here with you until you get out tomorrow," Twin said, checking his watch.

"I got a babysitter now?"

"Yeah."

"I'm grown, Twin. What the fuck I look like?" she screamed on him.

"You look like you need some new weave and a makeover," Twin joked before leaving.

156

Zels sat down near the TV and put it on ESPN with the remote. She could not believe he just came into her space and took over.

"Excuse me, I was watching that," she said, as he looked back.

"Ok," Zels replied, and turned his attention back to the TV.

Traina couldn't lie, she was super turned on by his swag and demeanor. She sucked her teeth, trying to get his attention. The first time didn't work, so she did it again.

"You got a flat tire," he asked.

"What are you talking about?" She said.

"This gonna be a long night. I am going to get me some coffee." Zels got up.

"Good, get me some creamer and no sugar Espresso, please." She snapped her fingers, making him laugh.

Romell Tukes

Chapter 31

North Philly

Sosa had been spending a lot of time with Karlee. He had even been going up to the college study hall building with her, just to spend time with her, and show her it was more than sex.

The way he made love to Karlee, he never felt with no other woman.

Around her, he felt as if he was in their own galaxy. She made him feel loved and cared for. Just looking at her did something to his ego.

He knew she was just what he really needed to balance his life and better himself.

Karlee talked to him about leaving the streets alone, but he would normally change the subject.

Stopping was something he didn't have in mind because he was just getting his feet wet in the game. Since dealing with his dad, he'd been seeing so much money. He had a few stash houses in Philly, and he told the only person he felt like he could trust about it, Karlee.

He wanted to grab a bite to eat from Max's, a Philly cheesesteak, up the street, on the next block, near the clock bar, a turn bar.

The Eagle Bar and the Max food spot were connected, so Sosa figured he would stop by the bar also, to catch a basketball game.

When he stopped at a red light, a black SUV with tints flashed its red and blue lights.

"Shit," Sosa cursed.

He pulled over and rolled down the windows on his Benz, turning down the music.

"Nice car." The cop was dressed in regular clothes, wearing Cartier frames and a gold Rolex watch.

When Sosa looked at the man in his face, he quickly recognized him from meeting with his brother, Block, before he killed him.

"Thanks, you should get one," Sosa shot back.

"If I was making as much money as you, I would, Sosa," Kilow stated.

"Who's Sosa?"

"Let's not play games, young bull. I did my research. You may fool the streets, but not me. I know all about you."

"Is that right?"

"Sure is," Kilow said with an evil smirk.

"So, what the fuck do you want? I know you have a lot of street rats who can help you out."

"I do, but I just felt like it was time we correctly meet. Who knows, maybe one day we can come together," Kilow said.

"I don't work with the police," Sosa shut his shit down. The look on Kilow's face said it all.

"You may not have no choice soon."

"When there's a will, there is a way," Sosa shot back.

"We'll see." Kilow walked off.

Sosa pulled off and drove home. He wasn't in the mood to eat or watch TV. He had bigger problems now.

***

Kilow drove back to the police station, thinking about what just happened at the traffic stop.

A few days ago, someone from Lil Hak's camp got booked with drugs and said Lil Hak worked for a nigga name Sosa, who drove a black Maserati SUV.

It wasn't hard for Kilow's detective skills to kick in at all. He needed to dig a little more into Sosa, but now he had a close eye on him. He was locked in.

***

West Philly

160

Foxy sat in her apartment, posting selfies on social media. She had over a few million followers on IG and was considered Insta-famous because of her exotic looks.

Since the death of Dawgg, she had been trying to figure some things out. She used to tell her brother to find a job and live life, so he could take care of his seed.

She saw so many people, friends and family, lose their life in the streets or go to prison, so Foxy never wanted Dawgg to fall victim.

Foxy always had a dream to live a normal life, coming from the worst section in West Philly. At times, she knew the reality of her life was to try to make it out the hood.

Foxy had a clique of girls, all known for getting to a bag. They did everything, modeling, club bottle girls, scamming, boosting and hustling.

The only thing she was against was stripping and selling pussy. Foxy disliked women who degraded themselves just for a dollar.

There were so many ways to get money and hustle. Why take the lazy way out? That was her mind frame.

Through the years, she knew a lot of people in higher places, before she rubbed shoulders with the right people.

She knew the Sosa Gang niggas had something to do with her brother's death, and she needed answers.

The only person she knew who would give her an answer was her ex-lover, Lez, the nigga whose name was tatted on her right ankle.

She would have to build up the balls and energy to ask Lez if he killed Dawgg, or knew who did. Word on the streets was there was a serious beef going on in Philly. She knew people who were scared to come outside. Some of her girls were scared to take their kids to school, it was so bad.

Foxy rolled up a blunt of sour diesel and got high all night.

Chapter 32

Temple Hospital, Philly

Zels stepped out of the hospital to take a smoke break. He really wanted to roll up a blunt of weed, but he knew he had to discipline himself until Traina was released.

Traina should be out in a few hours. The hospital staff kept her a little longer than they thought because they had to run more tests on her.

His time with Traina was great. She made him laugh and smile. They had a connection and a strong vibe with each other. He knew that was his boy's sister, but she was sexy, smart, and had a sense of humor. She had everything he looked for in a woman.

Zels stopped near a bench, where he saw a sexy chick, dressed in designer logos, sitting down, crying. The woman was a pretty, light skin bombshell.

Zels lit his cigarette and blew smoke into the air, looking at the woman's black swollen eyes, when she lifted her head, with tears rolling down her face.

"Naomi?" Zels said loudly, realizing who the woman was.

"Zels, hey," she replied with a dry and raspy voice from crying.

"You good?"

"Do I look good?" she asked, looking at him.

Zels didn't want to look too hard, but she looked like she got into a fight with a pro boxer. Naomi went to high school with Zels. The two were in a few of the same classes and were close. The last thing he heard about Naomi was she found some big time dope boy and had kids.

"What the fuck happened?" Zels didn't know what to really say or ask.

"My baby daddy and I got into it again, for the third time this week. I'm starting to be a regular here." She shook her head.

"You must like it then."

"What woman likes to get beat on? Are you serious, Zels?"

"Walk away," he suggested.

"Look at me. I'm living a good life, and my kids are good, so it's bigger than me. You know the game. I got everything I want and need, and more. Who wants a broke nigga? You know these niggas ain't on shit out here," she said.

"If that's how you carry it, then you made your own bed," Zels told her.

"This pussy so good niggas can't walk away. It's a curse and a blessing."

"I wish you luck, then."

"I gotta go pick up Sin's kids up from his mom's house on 5th and Moore in South Philly. But it was nice talking to you, Zels. You look good," she said, leaving.

"Who's Sin?"

"My abusive baby father," she said, getting into the back of a taxi.

Zels couldn't believe it. The nigga, Sin, who was his crew's rival, was her baby father.

While Zels stood there shocked, Traina came out from the slide doors with a fake attitude.

"Who da bitch?"

"Huh?"

"That bitch you were just talking to?" She sounded jealous.

"A chick I went to school with," he replied.

"Oh, my bad, playa."

"You play a lot."

"Whatever, I'm ready to go, ugly," she joked.

"I'ight, but first, fix your do-rag, looking like you about to go fight some project bitches," he shot back, laughing, as he walked to his car.

"It's a scurf, dummy."

"My bad."

"You're a mess, but I'm starving to go to IHOP."

"I'm down for dat," he said, placing her into his car, glad he was finally leaving. But he had Sin on his mind.

***

Sosa Gang

Downtown Philly

Barry watched his girlfriend Elina get ready for work as a paralegal for a big law firm. He stared as she slipped the dress over her phat ass.

He loved everything about Elina. She kept him young and full of fun. She was his eye candy.

"Make sure you behave until I get off. And we staying at the house, right? I mean I like the condo, but I love our home, and I decorated it," she bragged, filing her nails in their bathroom mirror.

When the two met at a basketball game, she thought he was a little older than her. But when she gave in to go on a date, she fell for his swag.

Elina had a good career. She was smart, beautiful, and his type. He loved his African American independent women.

"I will and I'll meet you at the house, baby."

"You sure?" she asked.

"Yes, sweetie. Just make sure you walk in the house ass naked like you did last time," he said, getting behind her, smelling her scent.

"I bet you would like it if I just walked in naked and did this." Elina turned around and dropped down to her knees, pulling out his hard penis. She sucked the tip, then worked her way down to the base, shoving it down her throat.

"Uhmmm shit." Barry closed his eyes and let her do her thing. Two minutes later, all his kids were down her throat.

"I'll see you for round two later," she said, getting up to leave.

Barry saw her walk out and wanted to stop her to fuck the dog shit out of her, but he let her go.

"Love you," he said, seeing the missed call from Sosa. Barry had been texted his son the addy so he could come through, an hour ago.

Romell Tukes

Chapter 33

Downtown Philly

Sosa traded in his SUV for an all-black Benz G550 truck, fully stocked with everything. The shit was clean. He'd never known his dad had a spot downtown, until now.

Getting out of the truck, he crossed the street. He noticed a pretty chick coming out of the building, looking like she was a businesswoman.

When he got closer, he saw the woman's face and realized it was Elina, his dad's girlfriend. Sosa wasn't surprised his dad had a bad bitch because he had a bag, but she did, too.

"Hey, Sosa," she stopped him, smiling excitedly to see him.

"Elina, how are you doing?" He replied, looking at her curves, and back to her pretty face.

"I'm good, on my way to work." She took a deep breath, as if it was a burden on her.

"Well, have a good day." Sosa turned to walk off.

"You, too."

Sosa turned to look back at her phat ass when he got in the building and knew she was the real deal.

Things with him and Karlee were great. She was everything he ever wanted in a woman.

His crew was going head up with the Outlaws, and shit was getting serious. Bodies were dropping. Money was still flowing, but the violence was still flowing, also, and it seemed the violence was on a rise.

Sosa made it to his dad's apartment door and knocked, until he heard his voice. Barry came to the door in a Versace sweat suit, with a blunt of weed he got from Cali, which was straight gas.

Barry smoked weed daily. It helped him focus and relax.

"What's up with you youngin? You look stressed out," Barry said.

"Not at all."

"Ok. What's going on? How's the product?" Barry asked, sitting down, grabbing an ashtray.

"No complaints."

"Guess that's good. But what you been doing? We need to spend some father and son time."

"Father and son time?" Sosa didn't expect to hear that.

"Yeah. You already took one son from me," Barry joked.

"I know you got more somewhere," Sosa shot back.

"Maybe."

"Do you remember da cop named Kilow, the same cop Block was dealing with?" Sosa saw a call from Twin but he left it in red.

"How could I forget? To be honest, I think one day he'll turn out to be a big pain in the ass," Barry said, knowing Kilow's type.

"Today may be that day. He recently pulled me over, talking shit, but I know he is about to be a problem," Sosa said.

"He wants a position or money?"

"I'm not giving him either one of those."

"Ok, so you know what needs to be done," Barry said.

"I know, but I'm weighing it out," Sosa said.

"That's on you. But sometimes in life, it's best to stop the cancer before it starts. That's an old school saying." Barry gave him a wink.

"Sounds like it."

"I have to go to Jummah (Muslim service). Maybe you should come," Barry offered.

"Nah, I'm good"

"You're not good until Allah says so."

"I feel you, but I have to go anyway," Sosa said, seeing Twin blow up his phone.

***

South Philly

Sosa pulled up on a side block next to 23rd street and Tasker, where it looked like a crime scene. Sosa placed his .44 S&W mag

168

revolver under his seat and called Twin, trying to figure out what was going on.

Sosa saw Twin across the street, so he got out of the car and hung up his phone.

"What's going on here?" Sosa started, looking at Twin.

"They just killed my brother in the store," Twin said.

"Damn, bull."

"It was that nigga, Crispy. They did a drive-by and killed three niggas, bro." Twin tried to control his emotions.

Even though he wasn't close to his brother who got killed, he was still his blood, so he took that to the heart.

"We're gonna spill some blood," Sosa said, watching the medical responders put white sheets over the dead bodies. The police picked up shell cases from a MP7 assault rifle.

Romell Tukes

Chapter 34

West Philly

Lez got a call from Foxy, asking him to meet her at the Gallery Mall, downtown.

He was on his way to the mall, hoping this meeting wasn't about the death of Dawgg, her brother.

Driving downtown, he thought about Twin's brother, who he saw on social media a few hours ago. Lez knew Twin was fucked up about his brother's death, even though Lez knew Twin's brother was a snake ass nigga.

There was so much going on in the city. Lez was running around gripped up with all types of guns: Freedom 380, Beretta 92-F, Mag 50, Cal Real tree Anaconda 44 mg, 9mm Luger SXT, and Glocks.

When he saw anybody from the Outlaws, he planned to treat them in broad daylight. Sosa wanted to have everybody to meet up again tonight.

Lez didn't want to beef. He just wanted to get money, but the ops were doing the most.

He had a half hour ride to the mall, so he played some old school Young Jeezy.

***

Downtown Philly

The Gallery Mall was called the Fashion District for its designer clothes and fashion stores.

Foxy tried her best to stay out of the Chanel and Dolce & Gabbana stores, but they were calling her name. She walked to the first level food court.

She saw dudes staring at her, but she rolled her eyes, paying them no mind at all.

The leather on her tight pants was hugging her ass and curves. She was looking like a snack on a dollar menu. Dudes couldn't help but stare, her sex appeal was on a thousand.

Calling Lez was one of the hardest things she'd ever had to do, but she needed answers. It wasn't like she was going to the police, she just wanted closure on her brother's behalf.

She saw Lez coming into the food court. When he got closer, she realized how long it had been since she'd seen her ex, and how good he looked.

All the thoughts of him cheating and hurting her started to hit her hard. Foxy also saw Lez kill a few people, which she didn't mind because she was used to violence, coming from East Philly.

"Hey, Foxy."

"Lez."

"How have you been? I don't get a hug?" Lez said.

"I'm good." She paid his remark no mind.

"What you been up to? I see you still looking good."

"I been living life," she replied.

"I bet."

"I called you out here for a reason." She started getting serious.

"What's that?"

"Somebody killed Dawgg," she said, looking into Lez's eyes, searching for any type of guilt.

"I'm sorry to hear that."

"You sorry?" Foxy caught an attitude.

"What else you want me to say?" he shot back, seeing Sosa calling him, but he didn't answer.

"It was your people, Lez. Come on, don't play games with me. Word on the streets is it was your crew, Sosa Gang."

"I don't know what you talking about."

"Lez, was it you?" She got teary eyed.

"Hell nah, Foxy. I would never cross you. I still care for you," Lez said.

"I hope you're telling the truth because someone is gonna pay for this, trust me. There are some things you don't know about me," she said.

"What does that mean?"

"You will see if you had anything to do with my brother's death," Foxy got up to leave.

Romell Tukes

Chapter 35

South Philly

Zels and Twin drove through the dark Philly Streets on their way to 5th Street to see if they could catch the bull, Sin.

When Zels told Twin about Naomi and what she told him, he was ready to slide. Twin was still heated over his sister being shot up.

The ride to 5th and Moore was silent because both men were in their zone. Twin had been seeing Zels and Traina getting real close lately, but he knew Zels was good people.

"Yo, I got holla at you, bull," Zels said, stopping at a red light.

"What's up?"

"Me and Traina have been kicking it, and I just felt I should let you know, bro. I know how you are behind her," Zels said, seeing his boy let out a laugh.

"I was waiting on you to tell me, my nigga. God damn," Twin replied.

"I had to wait for the right time. You know." Zels drove down 5th Street.

"Just don't hurt her because, if you hurt her, then you hurt me." Twin got real serious.

"I got you."

"I'ight, good. Now let's see if we can take this clown out the game, once and for all," Twin said as Zels parked, trying to see which crib stood out the most.

"You see the house with the two BMWs parked in the front?" Zels pointed out.

"Yeah." Twin could tell the crib Zels pointed out had some money, or somebody in there did.

"You want to try our hand?" Zels asked.

"You already know." Twin loaded his weapon, putting monkey nets on the end of his clip.

***

Naomi sat in the crib with Sin's mom, waiting on her baby to be dropped off by her mom.

Sin's mom was in the kitchen, cooking dinner for them.

"Naomi."

"Yes, Mom Dukes," Naomi yelled from the living room, knowing Sin's mom needed help.

"Can you help me cook this rice? Just put enough water in here so it can cook perfectly," Sin's mom stated.

"Ok." Naomi started helping out.

"That's too high," Sin's mom said, turning down the fire on the stove.

"Sorry."

"It's good, baby girl," Sin's mom stated.

The front door flew open and two gunmen busted inside, waving guns.

"Get down," Zels yelled to both women.

Naomi recognized Zels, and she couldn't believe it was him.

"Zels?" Naomi said before getting down on the kitchen floor.

"Where's Sin?" Twin asked the older, pretty woman, who he thought could be Sin's mom.

"My son ain't here."

"Where is he?" Zels asked, as he ignored Naomi's dirty looks.

"Zels, why are you doing this?" Naomi cried, as tears hit the floor.

"Bitch, why couldn't you just shut the fuck up?" Zels said, pacing back and forth.

Twin knew Sin wasn't there, so he was ready to bounce.

"We can't leave them here like this. They know your name." Twin gave him a look, letting him know what he had to do.

Naomi looked up at him with real puppy dog eyes.

"Zels, please don't," Naomi cried.

Zels pulled the trigger on Mom Dukes first, killing her with three shots to the chest.

Twin smiled as he thought about all of the homies lost, thanks to Sin's vicious attacks.

176

Naomi just knew she was next, but Zels looked at her, then back to Twin.

"Bro, I know her. She won't say a word, trust me," Zels said.

"I don't think this will be smart, Zels. What if she gets in her feelings one day and rats?"

Zels knew Twin had a point, but he fucked with Naomi.

"Let me be the judge of that. And if she does, I'll hold it down," Zels said, seeing Naomi say a silent prayer.

"Ok. That's on you. But when Sin get back, let your baby father know Sosa Gang stopped by, and let's keep it in the street," Twin said, walking out.

Zels saw Naomi's lips move, saying thank you.

"I'ma be in touch," Zels told her.

She nodded her head, moving away from the blood spill coming from Sin's mom's body.

***

Uptown Philly

Sosa and Lez were out and about, trying to find something to get into. A rap artist from Atlanta was supposed to come and perform at the Convention Center.

"I hate when it's nice out," Sosa said, driving through the main streets in his nice car.

"Nigga, you used to love the summer." Lez remembered Sosa used to have to the gang all over the place in the summertime, having fun.

They used to do shit like pool parties, amusement parks, house parties, out of town car shows, concerts, and any fun they could find.

"Back in the days, I did. Now, summertime is about who can rack up the highest body count," Sosa added.

"As long as we are up on the scoreboard," Lez joked, but was serious.

"Always, but you heard from Lil Hak?" Sosa asked.

"Nah, and that's a good thing. He's a fucking nut case."

"Shit, who ain't nowadays?"

"True," Lez stated.

"My pops has been looking out for work. I am keeping it real, bull. If he keeps coming how he is coming, we finna need to open up shop in New Jersey, Delaware, and outside of Philly," Sosa said.

"I know some people in Delaware and Jersey," Lez stated.

"Oh good. When we got our shit up, we are rocking out like that." Sosa was stuck in traffic because everybody was trying to get into the convention center parking lot, a block ahead.

"I'm all in, bro. But I heard Twin smoked Sin's mom last night, nigga."

"Twin ain't hit me in a few days," Sosa stated.

"He texted me this morning, telling me to watch the news. So, I put two and two together, but they left a witness," Lez said, shaking his head.

"They playing."

"Facts. Oh shit, I forgot to tell you, I ran into Foxy. Well, we met up."

"Trying to get that old joint back?" Sosa joked, knowing how deep they used to be.

"Nah, bro, it was about Dawgg, her late brother."

"I forgot her bro was an op."

"Yeah, man, I can tell she fucked up over it," Lez said.

"Fuck her."

"Yeah, I feel the same. But her words kinda shook me up, bro. You know how chicks be when they get all emotional and shit," Lez said.

"I don't think she's that type to go tell."

"I don't know, bull. Maybe, but she was acting and moving real funny."

"Does she know we did it?" Sosa asked, looking for a parking spot so they could catch the show.

"Yeah."

"Oh shit. Does she know who did it, or she just said the gang?"

"The gang. She threatened me lightweight, saying if she find out I had something to do with it, she would be disappointed." Lez ain't really want to say what he took from the convo, but he knew Foxy better than anyone, and she meant no harm, ever. She was a sweetheart.

"She'll get over it. Now, let's go turn up." Sosa parked and went to enjoy the rap concert.

Romell Tukes

Chapter 36

Downtown Philly

Kilow loved his days off. He would do shit that most cops wouldn't, like rob, kill, and sell drugs.

Two off duty cops drove in a Ford pickup truck behind him, ready for what the night had in store.

Kilow put Sosa to the back of his mind, for now, to focus on his new target, Lil Hak. For a few days now, he'd been watching Sosa, and he found nothing on him to make him think he was moving weight.

Lil Hak was a different story. He was out in Southwest stunting hard, in different cars, with 100,000 or better, a lot of jewelry, and his team of young wolves were eating.

Since they saw it as eating, it was time for Kilow to eat. Kilow's cousin had shit moving in Allentown and York for him. Whatever he would get from a lick, he would hit his cousin off.

The only thing Kilow was worried about was shit getting back to him, or his job, or the FEDS.

Tonight, they were going to Southwest to rob some local drug dealers, who worked for Lil Hak.

Kilow's crew of dirty cops were the real deal. He always locked in with crazy ass white boys, who'd been on the police force for a long time.

They crept to Southwest at midnight, on their way to Paschall Projects for their own raid.

***

Southwest Philly

Dex, Tray, and Milly all posted up in the trap, which was in the last building in the projects.

Paschall Projects had a high crime rate and was a heavy drug area. Niggas sold drugs together, in the hallways, out on the play-ground, on the basketball courts, and at all hours of the night.

Lil Hak ran the hood, with the help of his little cousin, Dex, who was about to turn twenty-one in 24 hours.

"This shit coming back good as hell," Tray yelled from the kitchen, cooking coke in the Pyrex pot, something he loved to do, since his mom taught him how to cook up work.

"Nigga, you supposed to be done. My nigga, you been cooking for three hours. My aunty about to come back any minute, dumb ass nigga," Milly shouted.

"I got five hundred, bro. Calm down, blood," Troy yelled.

"Nigga, what I told you about calling me blood? I'm a Philly bull, Sosa Gang. You da only blood gang member on this side, goofy," Milly replied, seeing Dex laugh.

Everybody in Philly was Muslim, Sosa Gang and Outlaw members. There were a few Blood gang members on the Westside.

"You have a lot of money you put in the safe because Lil Hak came through in the early morning," Dex said.

"I just put 12,000 in there that I got from House and Boosie," Milly shot back, playing on his phone.

"I'ight, so that's 150,000 max," he said to himself, walking into the kitchen.

Dex covered his mouth because he hated the smell of cooking crack. He felt that shit getting in his pores. Trey wore a mask and gloves while cooking.

There were two 45 colt desert eagles on the kitchen table, just in case a nigga tried their line.

The other day, Sosa Gang and the young Outlaw niggas had a big shootout in front of a Chinese store, killing a man from each crew in broad day light.

"I am going next door and getting some head from Hanna's fat ass," Max said.

"Hold up. I'm coming too," Milly said, knowing Hanna's head game was crazy. She was a fat bitch with a crazy dick sucking talent.

"Hell nah, bull. This ain't no party pack. And she told you not to come back because your dick stank," Dex joked on Milly.

"You bugging, my nigga," Milly said before, the front door got knocked off the door frame, and three men rushed in with guns.

Milly reached for the guns and got shot in the face.

Max saw Milly's body drop and pulled his gun, shooting back.

Boc. Boc. Boc. Boc. Boc. Boc. Boc.

Dex shot one of the cops in the neck, killing him.

Kilow shot at Dex and Tray, then rushed to save his fellow cop, who was already dead.

"Clean this shit out and call it in," Kilow told his boy, who searched for drugs and money.

They got the drugs and money, then called it in. when the police arrived, everybody was surprised to see a good cop, who was a vet on the force, dead.

Romell Tukes

Sosa Gang

Chapter 37

Southwest Philly

Lil Hak and a few of his goons drove dirt bikes down 62nd and Elmwood, on the way to meet with Roddy, who was down with the D.C. bulls.

D.C. was the nickname for a crew called Dream Chasers. They were the third largest clique in the city, and they didn't play any games.

Lil Hak and Roddy went to school together. But the main issue wasn't Roddy, it was Roddy's older brother, Wayne, who was locked up, fighting a body he caught last year in South Philly

The two crews didn't have beef at the moment. Sosa Gang fucked with a few D.C. niggas, but the Outlaws were there real ops.

Eight dirt bikes pulled up to the block to see Roddy and his crew outside, drinking and watching the Sosa Gang niggas. Everybody knew what type of bullshit they were on.

Roddy got out of his Lexus coupe with a thick bad bitch from out of town. She was a showstopper. This was Roddy's block, but he let his little brother run the show, while he was getting money out of town.

At 19 years old, he was playing with a big bag. He put his crew on, just like his brother, Wayne, used to do, before he caught his case.

Roddy knew Lil Hak real good when they went to middle school and high school together.

"Lil Hak, what up, young bull," Roddy approached Lil Hak as he got off the bike.

"Roddy, what's good, homie? I see you out here shining," Lil Hak looked at the chick, the car, and the jewelry he had on.

"Sumthin light, but what's da vibe? I know you ain't come to eye my bitch," Roddy joked.

"Nah, bro, I wanna form an ally with y'all."

"With us D.C.?

"Yeah, bro."

"I don't know. What Lez and Twin think about this? You know Lez and Wayne got their own little shit," Roddy said.

Lez and Wayne had fake beef over a bitch, nothing serious, but they had a bitter taste about each other.

"That shit petty, bro. We on money and trying to lock shit down, bull," Lil Hak told him.

"Facts. I've been hearing about y'all shooting shit up, fucking the city up," Roddy stated.

"We about to do big things soon, bro. And I know your crew and us will expand deeper than Philly," Lil Hak says.

"I been hearing about some nigga name Sosa from around this way, running the show?" Roddy asked, using the man's name to ring bells.

"That's the bro. He making big moves for us."

"That's love, and we need a plug, so let me holla at Wayne first," Roddy stated, liking what he was hearing. But he knew fucking with Sosa Gang would come with issues.

Two cars crept down the street without lights. Everybody was so focused on the conversion; they paid no attention to the two cars.

"Who dat?" Someone yelled, but it was too late.

Tat. Tat. Tat. Tat. Tat.

Bullets tore through the crowd, hitting Roddy's little brother and two more people on the block, as everybody panicked

Lil Hak and Roddy pulled out their weapons, shooting at the cars with Glocks, as they spinned off down the block.

"Forty," some chick yelled, seeing Roddy's little brother on the ground, bleeding to death, a few feet away from him.

When Roddy saw this, he spazzed out, and rushed to save his little brother. But the crowd knew he was dead.

Lil Hak heard sirens, so him and his crew jumped on their bikes, leaving the scene because they had guns on them. Lil Hak saw Crispy's ice grill hanging out the window, letting off shots from the AK 47 assault rifle with a hundred round drum.

Getting caught slipping on a Dream Chaser block could spark a new wave of killing in the city. Now Roddy's little brother got hit up.

Sosa Gang

***

South Philly

Crispy got rid of the two stolen cars him and his crew used to do the drive by, just minutes ago.

When he was driving through Southwest, he was going to speak to Roddy about getting down with his crew, the Outlaws.

Seeing Lil Hak and a few Sosa Gang niggas, he knew it was now or never to make a move on Lil Hak.

Crispy didn't give a fuck who he shot, when he got in kill zone. He as not worried about the D.C. bulls because he knew their team couldn't fuck with his, even though they had some hitters.

If anything, he was worried about Roddy and Wayne.

"Yo, Crispy," a little kid said, standing on 9th and Shink, close to midnight. Crispy knew the little kid, and his mom was a young crackhead and part-time hooker.

"What are you doing outside this late?"

"Mommy got two dudes in her bedroom, and she told me to get out until she's done," the kid said.

Crispy shook his head. He had a soft spot for little kids. He actually wanted a football team.

"Take this, little man." Crispy handed him two hundred dollars.

"Thanks, Crispy." The little kid ran up the stairs, to hide the money.

Romell Tukes

Chapter 38

Zels was entering Traina's new apartment, near 27th. The two of them had been vibing hard, going out to have fun, and out on dates, getting to know each other.

Zels never felt this way about a woman before. He was really feeling Traina because, not only was she beautiful, but she was smart, funny, and a real woman.

Approaching her door, he shook off his wet Prada raincoat because it had been raining all day.

Earlier, he bought her a nice heart necklace. She called him over so they could check out a new Ice Cube movie.

"Knock. Knock."

Zels was nervous every time he got near her. For some reason, he knew there were real feelings he'd been building for her.

"Zels."

She opened the door, wearing a dress with bare feet, showing her pretty feet.

"Hey, pretty girl," Zels walked into the nice apartment, seeing she'd hooked it up wall to wall.

"I'm glad you're here. I hope you're not hungry because I don't feel like cooking. But I will order you some food," she smiled.

"I'm ok, but I do have something for you," Zels took off his coat, hanging it on the hooks on the wall, and pulling out a black box.

"What's this?" She said, as he handed her the box.

"Open it, big head." Zels saw her eyes light up when she opened it.

"Oh my god, Zels, it is so nice." She rushed to give him a hug.

"You better slow down, you're still healing," he said, smelling her good perfume.

"Boy, shut up, and come to the room." She walked to the back, and Zels saw how her ass jiggled with each step.

"What were you watching?" He said, seeing her bend over in front of the large flat, TV, and grabbing the remote. He saw she had on no panties because her phat pussy could be seen.

Zels penis grew, as he stared for a few seconds, while taking off his designer shoes.

"An Ice Cube movie." She turned to him, jumping in her bed. She saw his cock poking out of his crotch, and she looked at him smiling, before resting her feet on his lap and getting comfortable.

"Traina, I want to be your man." He looked her in her eyes to see a surprised look.

"Let's take our time." She rubbed her feet on his cock.

"I'm with that." Zels knew what time it was. He reached in to suck on her neck, making her moan. He took her breasts out and tongued her nipples.

Zels stopped and got undressed. Her jaw dropped when she saw his masterpiece.

"Damn, Zels," she said, going into her own nasty thoughts.

She took his dick in her mouth, starting off slowly, working her juicy lips and tongue to the head of the shaft, before taking it down her throat.

Traina didn't like sucking dick, but she felt like he warned her. She managed to gulp down inch by inch, before she felt pre-cum spill out.

"Uhmmmm, hold up." Zels had to stop her and return the solid.

He laid her down, going down south to her pretty phat coochie that looked perfect and intact.

Zels buried his face between her thick thighs and went to work.

"Ohhhh, shit, baby," she moaned, as his tongue went crazy inside her warmth.

After the exquisite torture of his oral sex, he was ready to feel her sex box.

Zels got on top of her, looking into her eyes as he stuck his cock inside her tight pussy. She was horny and frustrated, wanting every inch in her walls.

"Fuck me, Zels. I need you," she cried out.

He pushed forward, slowly impaling her on the length of his massive rod. Once all the way in, she felt her climax. As he picked up the pace, the mattress squeaked and he thrusted into her.

Traina came hard, while he was pounding her pussy out.

Traina bent over, showing her big ass, wanting it doggy-style. And Zels had no problem filling her up.

Zels slapped her ass cheeks, which echoed through the crib, as he went deep in her. His thrusts clapped into her ass with every pound.

"Ohhh, Zels, yessss." She grabbed the nearest item to him, which was a pillow, as Zels gave her the best dick she'd ever had.

They made deep and passionate love all night, until they went to sleep. The next morning, Traina made it official by telling him he was her boo thang.

***

Uptown Philly

Sosa had recently got a new condo in a nice area for him to stay low at when shit got real, and to hide out.

Shit with Karlee had been going good. She had been talking about having babies and marriage, but he wasn't ready for that yet, and she disliked when he told her things like that.

He heard his buzzer ring, and he knew who it was, his dad. Sosa went to buzz his dad inside the crib.

Minutes later, Barry walked inside wearing an Islamic garment.

"I was on my way to the mosque when you called, son. What's going on?" Barry walked through the empty, nice pad.

"I ain't know what you wanted me to do with the money, and I don't like to talk over the phone," Sosa said.

"The same location as last time, and I'll assume your upping your count?"

"Yes." Sosa was ready for more drugs.

"Ok. I got you. But there is a kid named James, who goes by the name Sour, he's working for the police."

"How do you know all of this?" Sosa asked, knowing who Sour was. He was Lez's cousin from North Philly.

"I have my connects, but you need to tighten up," Barry said, leaving. Sosa sat down, thinking about how he was starting to have loose ends within the gang.

Chapter 39

West Philly

Lez parked in front of his cousin's building, hoping to make his way to the side alley leading towards the back.

Sosa called him earlier and informed him about some crazy news. He would've never been able to put two and two together.

In the back, an older, tall, dark-skin brother awaited him with a black bag, full of money.

"What's up, cuz?" Sour said, seeing there was something wrong with his body language.

"Nigga, you ratting." Lez pulled out his gun.

"What? Chill, cuz, you're tripping," Sour cried out, scared because he knew how Lez got down and, it wasn't nice.

"I heard you snitching," Lez said. He saw Sour's mom coming out of the back, surprised to see Lez pointing a gun at her son.

"Lez, what are you doing?" His aunty yelled out.

"This nigga trying to get me jammed up. He telling on me," Lez yelled.

"Sour, I told you not to go and snitch on your cousin. Now look at you," Sour's mom shouted.

"Mom, shut up," Sour said.

"What did you tell them?" Lez asked seriously.

"They wanted to know who were the leaders of Sosa Gang, and they asked about you and some murders," Sour said.

"Sour, I know you ain't doing your own cousin like that," Sour's mom said, who had been in the game for years. She'd sold drugs and did one or two things.

"Mom, they asked about you, too?" Sour stated.

"You what?" His mom looked at him as if he was crazy.

"I'm sorry, mama, but they're gonna raid the spot in a few days," Sour stated.

"You rat ass nigga, I should've swallowed your bitch ass. Lez, kill this nigga. I hate rats," Sour's mom walked back into the house, slamming the door.

Boc. Boc. Boc. Boc. Boc.

Lez killed his cousin and left him there. He knew his aunty was official. She hated rats, even if it was her own child.

***

South Philly

Crispy brought one of his new bitches to one of his traps. She had her head in his lap on the couch, giving him a sloppy blow job.

"Damn, bitch," he said, shooting a load into the back of her throat.

"You taste amazing." The woman raised up from his lap, like a zombie from the Walking Dead.

"What's your name again?" Crispy had met the chick earlier at a big cook-out in the uptown area.

"Oh my god, you can't be serious," she said, catching an attitude.

"At least I asked," he said, seeing a tattoo on her arm that said Lez.

"Valeria."

"Who name is that?" Crispy had a feeling something wasn't right.

"My ex-boyfriend. I hate that nigga," she said pissed off, thinking of Lez.

"What happened?" He asked, sounding concerned.

"He did me fucked up." Valeria got emotional quickly.

"Fuck that nigga. You got me, now," Crispy stated.

"I do?"

"Yeah, I'm here for you. I don't even like that nigga," Crispy stated.

"You know Lez?" she asked.

"Yeah, he killed my brother," Crispy said sadly.

194

"Damn, I'm sorry to hear that. I wish I could help somehow, babe," she said, rubbing on his private part.

"There is something, baby."

"Anything?" she said sexually.

"Can you find out where he be at?" Crispy gave her the sad face.

"I would love to help you," she said, pulling out his penis and sucking it slowly, up and down.

Crispy smiled, knowing Allah worked in mysterious ways.

***

Downtown Philly

A big rap concert was taking place at the Made of America Arena, and Lil Hak and Twin had both come out, shutting shit down.

With their crews together, they were a hundred deep. Plus, they had guns on them, just in case shit got crazy. Last year, two niggas got shot, and one was dead outside, after a shootout.

"Your boy, Lil Uzi, performing?" Twin asked Lil Hak, as they had a big section on the lower level.

"He up next," Lil Hak said, as the rapper from New York, A Boogie Wit Da Hoodie, turned up the crowd.

"What's up wit them D.C. niggas? I heard they fucking with us," Twin asked, referring to the rumors he'd been hearing about D.C. and the Sosa Gang niggas tag teaming.

"Yeah, they fucking with us, bro. I facetime Sosa, and he was down," Lil Hak had to whisper in Twin's ear, due to the loud music playing.

"I fuck wit Wayne and Roddy, so that will be a good look. But you can't really trust them bulls. They got some shady ways," Lil Hak said.

"Don't we all," Twin laughed.

When the concert was over, Twin's little homie saw Sin and a gang of niggas near gate six, and told Twin.

In a matter of seconds, a big shootout broke out, and five people got hit up, two died, and nine people got arrested at the scene.

Twin, Lil Hak, and Sin all lost men from each side, but they made it out safe.

Chapter 40

Downtown Philly

Sosa took an Uber to the bike store to cop a bike for the summer. He wanted a ninja sports bike. He liked dirt bikes, but he was on his grown man shit.

Sosa was hearing about the crazy shootout at the concert yesterday. One thing for sure was Sosa always kept his car to the street.

When he heard it was Sosa Gang v/s Outlaws, he knew that would draw heat to him and the crew.

The drugs he was getting from his pops were moving fast, so fast that Barry was having a hard time keeping up orders. Last night, when he went to see his dad, Barry's girlfriend gave him a hug, slightly rubbing on his manhood.

Sosa knew he wasn't tripping about her sexual looks and body language, but he would never cross the line, even though Barry's girl was a bad bitch from head to toe.

After he paid for his bike, he wanted to pop up on Karlee at her college, since he was close. Sosa was really into it. There was something so special about her that he couldn't resist, at all.

Sosa had already pre-ordered his motorcycle, and it was waiting for him in the front. It took just minutes to get the tags and the correct paperwork.

"It's on now." Sosa placed his helmet on and took off down the block, loving the power the bike had. He went to Karlee's school, which only took a few minutes to get there.

***

Temple University, Philly

Karlee was exhausted to the max, after taking three exams this morning.

She had a few more classes, but first, she wanted to go grab some lunch alone real quick.

The thought of Sosa crossed her mind and made her smile hard. Walking to her car, she thought her eyes were playing tricks on her when she saw a man on a motorcycle with pink roses.

"Babe," she yelled, running to Sosa on a motorcycle.

"Hey, beautiful." Sosa got off the bike as the sunshine gleamed off his bust down watch.

"These are for me? Oh my god." Karlee loved the way Sosa treated her and the way he catered to her needs and wants. She heard other women's stories of how bad their loved ones treated them, and it made her stomach sick.

"Of course."

"When you get this?" She asked, looking at the bike.

"Just now. Facts. You like?"

"No, it's dangerous."

"You saw my sister today?" Sosa asked because he hadn't heard from her in days.

"I saw her earlier, before she left with Rexa."

"Who dat?"

"Some chick I don't like," Karlee said, smelling the roses.

"Where were you going?"

"Out to eat," she shot back.

"Can I come?"

"Sure but leave the bike and get in my car. We out baby," she said, getting in her car. They enjoyed the day out, until she had to go back to school.

***

Downtown Philly

Lez got a call from his ex-girlfriend, Valeria, asking him to meet her at Chart House, a restaurant.

When he got the call, he was going to block her, but she told him she had some very important information for him.

Lez wanted to know what she had to say to him.

Pulling into the lot, he didn't see Valeria's car anywhere in sight, but he figured he was there early.

Parking next to an SUV, he saw the restaurant was packed from the outside. He called Valeria, but for some reason, her phone went straight to voicemail.

Lez had to take a piss anyway, so he figured by the time he came out, she would be there, or on her way. Later, Lez had to go to Delaware to get up with his cousins out there to put them on a bag.

Getting out, he saw people leaving the food spot. One of the dudes he saw, named Itman, was from South Philly and down with the D.C. clique.

Lez didn't mind the two crews having an alliance, but he hated Wayne. The two used to fight daily, and even had a shootout over a bitch.

Tat. Tat. Tat. Tat. Tat. Tat. Tat. Tat. Tat. Tat. Tat. Tat. Tat. Tat. Tat. Tat. Tat. Tat.

Bullets came from all over the place, as he took cover and went for his weapon to fire back.

Bloc. Bloc. Bloc. Bloc. Bloc. Bloc. Bloc. Bloc. Bloc.

Lez hit one of the shooters in his face, while the other four tried to take his head off.

Itman took the lead from across the lot and helped Lez against his ops.

Boom. Boom. Boom. Boom. Boom. Boom.

"It's them Outlaws niggas," Itman yelled, firing a few shots into the man's chest, knocking the man off his feet.

Lez and Itman reversed the gunman's plot and started to take them out.

In a matter of seconds, the rest of the gunman laid on the ground in red puddles.

People ran inside, calling the police, praying the men didn't come inside and start shooting shit up.

Lez gave Itman a thank you look before he climbed into his car, pulling off. Lez was far from dumb, he knew Valeria set him up because she was nowhere in sight.

Romell Tukes

Chapter 41

Southwest Philly

Sosa got a call from Lil Hak earlier, asking him to meet with Roddy, who had been requesting to speak to him. Since the Sosa Gang was rocking with the D.C crew, he didn't mind at all.

Word on the street was spreading quickly about how the teams were coming together to take over the city. There was a few little other crews scattered around the city, but they were all scared to death of both crews.

He drive down 73rd Street in his get around car, which was a Dodge Challenger SRT Demon 2-door coupe. Sosa loved the crazy horsepower the car had, when he pressed the pedal.

Roddy was posted up next to a black Range Rover SUV with rims. Sosa always heard of Roddy and Wayne. They had a crazy body count, also.

"Roddy, what's going on, bull?" Sosa climbed out, tucking his gun on the dangerous block Lil Hak ran. But he still was the man behind the scenes, so not too many people knew who he was, besides the main hitters.

"I ain't seen you in a while, bro," Roddy embraced Sosa.

"Facts. But what's going on with your brother's case?"

"I don't know yet. He is waiting now, dealing with court and shit," Roddy told him.

"He got a lawyer?"

"Yeah, that's taken care of," Roddy assured him.

"I'ight good. That's what's up. I wish him the best. But it's good to have you and your crew join the family."

"Likewise, bro. But I needed to speak to you about something," Roddy said, seeing he had Sosa's full attention.

"What's going on?"

"I need a plug, bro. I know y'all doing y'all one two and me and my guys trying to eat."

"Say no more, I got you, bro. Give me a few days," Sosa stated.

"You sure?"

"All I got is my word, bro. I got you," Sosa assured him.

"Ok."

"I'll have Lil Hak get with you, and I'll bless you, bull," Sosa told him, before leaving.

Roddy was glad because he didn't have any drugs, and his wolves were starting to howl. He planned to tell Wayne about this down the line. But as of now, he saw big money. Everybody knew how Sosa Gang was flooding the streets with the best product, just like Block used to do, before he got killed.

***

Cherry Hill Mall, NJ

Zels has been kicking it so hard with Traina, he hadn't been in the field or around the gang too much. He drove out twenty minutes to a big mall outside of Camden, NJ

He was shopping, hitting up a few big name stores, like Gucci, Prada, and Fendi. He was also getting some things for his new girl-friend, Traina. He knew her size and everything, so he was good.

As he walked into Macy's to use the restroom, he paused when he saw Naomi walking out.

When they locked eyes, Naomi froze, knowing what he did to Sin's mom a few weeks ago.

"Naomi, hey," he said, breaking the ice and weird vibes.

"Hey," she stated in a dry voice, looking down at the floor.

"Are we good?"

"Of course, we are always good, handsome. But you caused me a lot of stress because Sin thought I had something to do with what happened," she told him.

"What did you tell him?" Zels hoped she told Sin it was his crew.

"The same thing I told the police. I was in the bathroom. I don't know what happened. I just saw her in a puddle of blood after I heard gunshots," she said.

"Thanks."

"He said something about the Sosa Gang doing it and how he did not know why I was still alive." She smiled before frowning.

"Are you safe?"

"Yes, Zels, but you're not. He's crazy, Zels, and I don't want to see you on the news, or my baby father." Her facial expression looked saddened.

"I feel where you're coming from," he said, seeing Traina call his iPhone.

"That was your girlfriend that day at the hospital, Zels?"

"Something like that."

"Oh. Well, I wish you luck. I'ma getting going," she said, disappointed he had a girl.

"Ok. Call when you need me," Zels said, walking off and rethinking his conversation.

Romell Tukes

Chapter 42

Southwest Philly

Zarhya and her good friend, Rexa, went out to a bar on 72nd and Woodard, called Happy End.

"That's your sixth drink, girl. Don't forget you have to go to school and study, bitch. You up here getting litty," Rexa said, laughing, as they sat at the bar next to a bunch of cops, who were getting off duty, having some drinks.

"I thought you were meeting your date here?" Zarhya asked.

"I am, girl. He should be getting off early," Rexa said, looking around.

Rexa was a medium height beauty, with a phat ass and no stomach. She got her body done last year by an older dude she was fucking, who had money.

"You tripping. You need to slow down," Zarhya told her because she knew how her friend was a thot.

"I'm living."

"If that is living, I hate to see what it would be like to be down bad," Zarhya joked.

"Here he go," Rexa said, as a handsome man walked up to them.

"Hey, ladies," the man said.

"Hey, baby," Rexa kissed his lips, as Zarhya shook her head.

"I'm Zarhya."

"I'm Kilow."

"Kilow, like the drugs?" Zarhya thought Rexa found another drug dealer.

"No, that's my last name," Kilow said, dressed in regular clothes.

"Oh," Zarhya said.

"My man got a good job, girl," Rexa bragged.

"Is that right?"

"Yes. I'm a cop," Kilow said.

"A cop? Wow, that's nice."

"You don't know the half," Kilow replied.

They had a few more drinks and enjoyed the evening with each other, on their three wheel date.

***

Downtown Philly

Twin drove to the Marriott hotel to meet a woman named Amberly, who he bumps into a few days ago in North Philly at a store.

Things had been heating up the past couple of days in Philly. Niggas were dying left and right, non-stop, and it was thanks to the Outlaws and D.C. going at it, with his gang's help.

Everybody in the streets knew he killed Dawgg. That was the new gossip of the town, but Twin didn't give a fuck. It was on sight with any Outlaw nigga he saw.

Twin's dad spoke to him today in the Mosque, when he went to Jummah Friday services.

His pop told him what good it is to have everything in life, but in the hereafter, you have nothing, not even your deeds and honor because you did nothing to earn it.

Hearing that made him think all day about changing up his way of living and start back focusing on his deen.

Pulling up to the hotel lot in his new Mercedes-Benz SL550 coupe candy red fresh off the lot, he felt like he was a man.

South Philly was getting so much money now, he only felt it was right to get a big bag. It was well deserved.

Texting Amberly, he wondered where she was at. But he figured he could pay for the hotel room before she got there.

When Twin was exiting his Benz, he figured it would be safe to leave his pistol in the car.

He looked to his right saw two beautiful women coming towards him, and one of them was Amberly

"Amberly," Twin said, approaching her in the middle of the parking lot.

Twin saw something was totally off about the look on their faces, and when he got closer, he knew why.

Both women pulled out a Glock 45 with thirty shot clips attached to it and started letting off like professional shooters.

Bloc. Bloc. Bloc. Bloc.

Twin got low down between two cars, as bullets bounced off of car windows and mirrors. Twin couldn't believe he was being ambushed by two women, two sexy chicks at that.

He patted himself down, looking for a weapon he forgot in his car.

"Twinnnnnnnnn," Amberly yelled out like a madwoman.

Twin saw his car a few cars down the row, and he knew it was his only chance, so he took it. He ran to the Benz. Bullets were fired at him, but luckily none hit him. He hopped in his car, hitting the push-to-start button, and swerving off, hearing live rounds hit his car. He knew someone else was behind this because it was well planned, and he knew Amberly was slow, just after a few conversations with her.

Romell Tukes

Chapter 43

South Philly

Somewhere on 27th and Reed, in the basement of a two story house, on a block full of row houses, Sin and Crispy sat alone, off to the side, while their crew shot dice on the wall.They were loud as hell.

"Did you pay off the cop nigga from the 26th District?" Sin asked.
"Who, Galdwin?" Crispy shot back, as he took a sip of liquor.

"Yeah, bull, who else?" Sin hated when people asked dumb shit. That was one of his pet peeves.
"Yeah, bro. I saw him two nights ago downtown in Center City." Crispy rolled up a blunt.
"How the fuck did these two niggas come together, bull? They got us in numbers, but will never have us in heart." Sin showed no signs of weakness, when he spoke like that.
"Ten wolves will always run through a hundred sheep," Crispy stated.
"I agree. But them niggas up on the scoreboard. We losing family and friends," said Sin.
"I got a plan, but it's gonna take some time to put together," Crispy said.
"Do your thing, bull. I gotta slide." Sin saw his baby mother, Naomi, texting him for money.
"The limits of your mind are the limits you create. You are your only opponent," Crispy said, when Sin got up.
"That's the smartest shit you said all day," Sin laughed, leaving with four goons.

***

German Town, PA

Outside of Philly was a small town called German Town, where Valeria grew up with her mother, who was a hard working school bus driver for a middle school.

Valeria was driving to her mom's job to pick her up because her car was in the shop.

She felt bad for setting Lez up, but she had a heart full of venom. Hearing Lez didn't get killed crushed her heart because she knew how dangerous he was.

When she stressed to Crispy about how serious Lez was, he laughed and gave her a bullet proof vest and a gun. Then he kicked her out the crib. And to make shit worse, he blocked her number.

Her mom's job was next to a park, where she used to go as a child after school.

Parking in front of her mom's job, she came out seconds later.

Valeria got out to help her mom place her work bags in the trunk of her two-door Acura.

"You've been working out, baby," her mom said, seeing how buff her daughter looked under her Amiri T-shirt.

"No."

"Well, what's that?" Her mom touched her vest.

Her Mom was a God fearing, church woman. She did her best to keep her two boys and baby girl away from the crazy streets.

"It's a vest." Valeria was catching an attitude.

"Why you wearing it?"

"Mom, can we just go please?" Valeria said, closing the trunk, and seeing a motorcycle pull up with a tall man on it.

Something about the man on the bike made her do a double-take. She was glad she did a double-take because she saw the man lift a weapon.

Tat. Tat. Tat. Tat. Tat.

A bullet hit Valeria in her chest, but three bullets entered her mom's breast, knocking her in the air and onto the ground.

"Mom," she yelled, as the bike drove off.

People ran outside to help. They dialed the police number, trying to help their coworker, who was on her last breath.

Valeria yanked off her vest, feeling winded, but the bullet she caught didn't go through the vest.

***

Temple Hospital, Philly

Valeria sat in the hospital in tears, seeing the doctor, who worked on her mom, walk off with the pink papers in her hand, which were the deceased papers.

The doctor told her they tried to save her mom, but she didn't make it because the bullets hit too many main organs.

While Valeria was crying, two cops entered the waiting room.

"Excuse us, but are you the one who was involved in the shooting at the school bus place in Germantown?" Kilow asked.

Since he was nearby where the shooting took place, he got assigned to the case.

"Yes, my mom is dead." Valeria cried like a newborn baby.

"I'm sorry to hear that, but we can help find whoever did this. Help us bring peace to your mother," the other cop stated, smiling lightly.

"Lez did it. Lez. Lez. I hate him. He killed my mom. I saw him," she yelled, while crying.

Kilow felt his heart stop and knew his brother fucked up again.

"We gonna get him," Kilow said. He told his partner to go home. He was going to take care of it.

"I hate him," Valeria cried, as Kilow stayed to comfort her for a while.

"Let me walk you outside. You need to get home." Kilow helped her up and took her outside. He guided her to her car and watched her drive off.

Kilow rushed to his car and followed Valeria. When he saw her car stop at a red light, he snuck up on the side of her driver side window.

Boc. Boc. Boc. Boc.

Bullets shattered Valeria's window hitting her in the face, neck, and ear. Kilow drove off, calling it in as if he heard gunshots. He used his personal gun, which he'd bought off the streets.

Chapter 44

Wilmington, Delaware

Lez drove out to see his cousins, who were in Delaware getting a little money. But he had plans to put them on a big bag.

His brother Kilow had been calling his phone all day, but Lez didn't feel like being bothered with Kilow's bullshit. He knew his brother like the back of his hands, and he always had a hidden agenda with him.

The only time he saw Kilow now was at family reunions, and driving by chasing criminals, mainly his Sosa Gang boys.

What Lez didn't understand was why Kilow had a hard on for his crew, especially the top members. A few weeks ago, Lil Hak was complaining about how Kilow was on his line.

The highway was long country roads with a 36 mph speed limit for the drivers.

Lez thought about the last talk he had with Foxy. He saw something in her eyes he'd never seen before, pain, hurt, and grief.

He got off the exit, using the GPS in his Mercedes-Benz truck. His cousins, Pico and Geek, were two burnt out, young, crazy niggas, living day for day, in the streets.

Driving into a small trailer park area with a few houses on the outside, he saw niggas outside deep.

Pico and Geek were posted up on a basketball court with their crew, watching a dog fight. Geek and his brother, Pico, had their hands in dog fighting, gun selling, and were the main source of product in the city.

They ran the city with their crew. Wilmington had a lot of money in there, and Pico and Geek wanted to lock it all down.

Lez climbed out of the truck with his iron tucked in his waistband. No matter where he went, he always had that gun on him because he knew Philly niggas were the most hated in certain areas, especially a nigga getting money.

"Oh shit, cuz, here," Geek shouted to Pico, who was talking to a thick, cute, brown skin chick from the hood, arguing with him about paying for her abortion.

"What's going on out here, player?" Lez asked Geek, seeing Pico on his way over, shaking his head.

"Same shit, trying to run it up," Geek said.

"Pico, what's up," Lez stated.

"I see you pulling up big?" Pico took a look at Lez's G-Wagon parked next to his Hellcat.

"Something light, bull. But I need to holla at y'all, cuz," Lez told them both, as the crowd on the basketball court grew loud, seeing one of the pit bulls kill the K-9 dog.

"We here to listen," Pico said.

"I'm in a good position now, and I want to see y'all eat. I want to flood Delaware, wit y'all help," Lez said.

"We are the city. But we are already doing it big, brother. We got a plug," Geek said.

"Damn, already?"

"Yeah, it's money to be made out there," Pico said.

"Last time I came out, y'all ain't have no plug. Now y'all up. I'm proud of y'all," Lez said.

"True," Pico shot back.

"Who supplying y'all?" Lez wondered.

"Kilow," Geek said.

"Who?"

"Your brother," Pico said, seeing the crazy look on Lez's face.

Lez had no clue his brother was moving weight. He wondered what Kilow was really up to now.

***

Miami, FL

Sosa and Twin went out to Miami for the weekend to celebrate Twin's birthday. They were in the mall, doing some shopping for an all red party in one of the biggest clubs in the city, called V-Live.

"You told Lil Hak you were coming out here?" Twin asked Sosa, walking into a jewelry store.

"Hell nah, how about you?" Sosa knew for a fact, if Lil Hak found out they went to the 305 without him, he would spazz out.

"Fuck no, bull. You know he would've caught that next flight, bull," Twin replied, looking at some Rolex watches and GIA certified diamond earrings.

"I went to speak to Roddy, and I'm feeling bro vibes. I'm starting to hit his hand, so his crew can eat. Plus, it will be a good way to network across the city," Sosa said.

"We need dem niggas," Twin said.

"We don't need nobody. We really all we got," Sosa corrected him.

"That's a fact," Twin said, looking at a sexy woman in a tight dress, who was looking at some bracelets.

"Damn." Sosa saw the woman from behind.

"Her ass is crazy, and she's bad," Twin said, deciding whether he should approach the woman.

The sexy redbone woman turned around and looked at Sosa, as if she knew who he was.

"No way that's her." Sosa was caught red handed, staring at her phat ass.

"Sosa," Elina yelled, rushing to give him a hug.

"Elina, how you doing?" Sosa wondered what his dad's girlfriend was doing in Miami, but he knew she did a lot of traveling.

"I'm good, out here for a few days, enjoying Miami. How about you, handsome?" Elina couldn't stop smiling at him, and Twin saw it, also. So, he walked off, letting them vibe.

"I'm chilling," Sosa couldn't help but to look at her titties and pierced nipples.

"How about you call me later and we can link up at my hotel, just as I've been waiting for the perfect opportunity," Elina's voice got sexy.

Elina took his phone and entered her number in it, before walking out, swaying her hips.

"You know her?"

"Long story. Let's shop so we can leave to get ready for this all red affair." Sosa started thinking about how crazy Elina was, and how he had no plans on calling her.

Chapter 45

Southwest Philly

Jummah Friday on 67th and Woodland was the Mosque to be at on Fridays. Muslims just walked out the packed Mosque, flooding the streets, leaving, talking, and some conducting business, legal and illegal.

Lil Hak saw Big Chev inside and they'd been cool for years now. Even though both men were born Muslims, they let the street life put them one foot in and one foot out of the religion.

Lil Hak made sure he made his five (Salat) prayers a day and fasted during the month of Ramadan. He wasn't a perfect Muslim by far, but he was striving.

"As-Salaam-Alaikum, big bro," Lil Hak embraced Big Chev with a tight hug. The two men went way back, just like Lez and Big Chev did.

"Wa-Alaikum-Salaam," Big Chev replied, with a big smile on his face.

"Where is the bull, Lez, at?" Lil Hak asked.

"I don't know. I'm supposed to meet him later at that new club near Center City," Big Chev said, seeing two beautiful Muslim women coming across the street, dressed in garments, covering their faces, with hijabs showing only their eyes.

Lil Hak saw the women fondling with something under their garments. Then he saw the Dracos come out.

Tat. Tat. Tat. Tat.

Big Chev got hit twice, as Lil Hak hit the ground, pulling out his heat and firing back, hitting one of the women.

The crowds of Muslim men, women, and kids took cover, yelling, trying their best to avoid being shot.

The women holding the Dracos continued to finish Lil Hak's career, but he was moving too fast. When she realized he was too swift, she took off, trying to get away from the scene, where she left two dead, Big Lak and an older gentleman, who was out trying to sell Muslim oil to feed his family.

Lil Hak saw Big Chev's dead, bloody body, and slid off to his car. Whenever he came to Jummah, he came to download, but he knew better now. He called Lez to tell him what had just happened to his best friend.

***

Downtown Philly, Days Later

Sosa was in his condo with his feet up, watching TV, laughing at the funny movie. Funny movies or real life gangsta movies, he liked to watch, unlike Karlee, who watched love movies all day, which bored him.

Since coming back from Miami, he heard about Big Chev's death, and it touched him because they chilled a few times, and Sosa liked his energy.

Sosa knew, one day, a person could be here, and the next day, they could be gone. He wanted to throw a big cook-out next weekend, just to bring his guys closer and do something for the city because school was starting back up soon. So he wanted to do something big. He felt like it was time for Philly to really know who Sosa was, the man behind the scenes. He knew the people would expose him more than he already was now.

Karlee walked in with some bags in her hands.

"Bae," she yelled, rocking Chanel everything.

Sosa loved her because he knew, if he didn't have a dime, she would be there for him still, unlike most women, who would run like a track star if shit got a real.

"Hey sweetheart." Sosa kissed her lips.

Since living with a woman, Sosa learned how to be more patient because, at times, she would drive him crazy.

"I want to cook for you, then do that thing you like with my tongue," she said.

"Ok. I'ma go wait for you."

"I wanna eat your ass baby," Karlee laughed.

"Karlee, don't play. I'll choke the shit out your ass." Sosa walked off.

"Just testing you, baby," she joked before starting their meal.

***

North Philly

Lil Hak and a van full of goons posted up in a section called Badlands, waiting for Amberly. Lil Hak did some serious research on Amberly and just as fate would have it, one of his little homie's girlfriends knew Amberly.

When he had his people do some digging, he found out Amberly was in a serious relationship with a man named Fight, who was Puerto Rican and getting a shit load of money.

Badlands was mostly Puerto Rican niggas, getting money, and Lez and the D.C. crew had this side on lock.

"These niggas getting money, bull," one of Lil Hak's shooters said, seeing cars pulling up left and right, buying drugs, as dealers went up to the window to serve them.

"That's them, Hak," DJ said. "The girl is the one who knows Amberly."

***

Amberly and Fight parked next to a corner store, and they both got out to go inside.

Fight owned the store, but he used it as a front to get drugs in from PR. He sold weight and had a crew getting money for him.

He'd been fucking with Amberly for a few weeks now, and she was starting to run a dent in his pockets, so he had plans to kick her to the curb in a few days. The pussy and head was off the hook.

Walking into the store, they went to the back to check on the money in the safe he had there.

Amberly took a seat as Fight did his thing, unlocking the safe to get the money out.

Boom.

The door flew open, and Fight reached for his gun in the safe. But his clever idea was put to an end.

Bloc. Bloc. Bloc.

Fight's body collapsed, and Amberly just sat there, unfazed.

"Am I supposed to yell, don't kill me? I only fear Allah," Amberly told Lil Hak and his goons.

"Today you gonna meet fear because I will make sure you meet Allah," Lil Hak said.

"Thank You," she replied.

"Take that money," Lil Hak told his goons, looking at the safe.

"I almost had you and Twin," she said.

"Me? Oh, that was you, little bitch?" Lil Hak slapped her so hard with the gun that she flew to the floor, looking dead.

"Fuck you, nigga." She slowly got back on her feet.

"I hate to kill a sexy bitch." Lil Hak looked at her curves.

"My time is up anyway. But you will be with me soon," she added.

"You think so?" Lil Hak saw a smirk on her face, but he knew the death games people played to save their life.

"Foxy been sending us to you, and trust me, she won't stop until y'all pay for Dawgg's death," said Amberly, as blood leaked down her face, like sweat after a long run.

"Foxy?" Lil Hak only knew one Foxy, and she was Dawgg's sister, but killing or the streets wasn't her field,

"Yep, now hurry up, so I can get this shit over with," she cried.

"I never saw such a beautiful woman in a rush to die," Lil Hak laughed, seeing her tears form.

"I've been living with HIV for five years now, and I can't take it anymore. The meds are making me more depressed," she cried, showing emotion and fear for the first time.

"At least you can take a load off," he stated.

Bloc. Bloc. Bloc.

He killed her and walked out, calling Lez, whose phone went to voicemail. He knew this threw a monkey wrench in the game.

Chapter 46

Downtown Philly

Barry had Elina's legs spread open in their king size bed. He found her entrance and slid as much of his rod as the position allowed into her tight pussy.

"Uhmmmm," she moaned, as he stroked slowly in and out of her drenched pussy, full of cream.

Barry loved the sensation of being inside her, as he humped her faster and faster. Her gushy sex box could be heard throughout the room.

"Yes, baby, harder. Fuck this good pussy," she shouted, as his nuts slapped against her swollen clit gently each time he thrusted his cock in her.

Elina was getting closer to orgasm with each stroke. But before she could get her rocks off, he shot off a load in her.

Barry switched positions and bent her over on all fours.

He slid his cock into her gently, in and out of her, speeding up his thrusts. Barry went as deep as he could in her pussy, hitting the bottom of her vagina, making her go crazy.

They fucked for twenty more minutes, then talked about plans for a vacation soon to Aruba.

***

North Philly

Foxy had been trying to take a nap all day but couldn't because the news she recently got of her home girl Amberly being killed crushed her.

If she would have known Amberly couldn't handle herself, she could have sent someone else to handle Sosa Gang.

When Amberly told her she missed her targets twice, with Twin and Lil Hak, she knew better than to send Amberly to line up Fight.

Luckily, she had a lot of ruthless friends, ready to kill at the drop of a dime for her.

Foxy came up with a plan so she could let Dawgg rest in peace, once and for all.

Foxy had a bloodline full of gangster in her, and she had the mind frame of a brilliant criminal. There were a lot of things Foxy had to keep a secret for a long time, but she knew soon it would all be exposed.

**

Downtown, Philly

Zels just arrived at FDC Philly, which was a federal holdover for federal inmates. Zels' uncle had been in there for seven years now, fighting a serious case.

His Uncle Tame was selling guns all throughout Philly, but he got a very big head and started slipping.

One day, he went to sell some weapons to a man he met days prior at a gas station, and shit went left real quick.

The man Tame met was a federal agent, and when Tame realized it was a setup, he killed the federal agent in broad daylight. Tame went on the run to North Carolina for a month, until he got caught for killing another man in a robbery.

Now Tame was awaiting trial, and he had the death penalty on him.

Zels was searched and taken to a booth, where the controlled visits for high profile or SHU inmates were held.

Growing up, Tame raised Zels, and he taught him the game, so Zels never forgot that. He made sure his uncle was good while locked down. Zels sent him money, pics, women to visit him, books, and whatever else he required.

Mainly, Tame wanted Islamic books because he was heavy on the deen. He was a faithful Muslim.

While waiting, he thought about his baby, Traina, who probably was still asleep at 10 a.m.

The love connection with them was going good, but Zels was ready for kids, and she wasn't. He felt like she was the one.

Minutes into his thoughts, Tame walked out, looking stocky in his jumpers. Tame was a tall, dark skin, ugly brother, with a bald head and big beard.

"As-Salaam-Alaikum." Tame's voice was deep

"Wa-alaikum-Salaam," Zels replied.

"Been hearing a lot about the crew in here, but you need to cut back and wise up," Tame said.

"I got you, Uncle. But how's everything?"

"I'm blessed, brother. Focus."

"I'ight good. I wish you were out. Shit rough," Zels said.

"I know, youngin. But you gotta stay on the straight path. The streets are about to get worse, especially when OG Kane gets back out there," Tame stated.

"OG Kane?" Zels asked. He'd heard the name many times, but it didn't click.

"He was down for twenty, about to touch the pavement, and the bull seriously controlled Philly for a long time, and killed half the city back in the day," Tame told him.

"Damn. Well, it's a new era," Zels said.

"Kane doesn't care about that, though, trust," Tame said.

"When you go back to court?"

"Soon, but it's not looking good." Tame was honest. They talked for twenty-five more minutes.

After the visit, Zels called Traina as he walked up to the car lot, but she wasn't picking up.

Walking through the lot, he didn't see the shadow appear from out the cut.

Boc. Boc. Boc. Boc. Boc. Boc. Boc. Boc. Boc. Boc. Boc. Boc.

Zels went down on his knees, first, as the bullets pierced his lower back.

Zels turned around and saw Sin standing over him, aiming his weapon at his face, and firing around into his face.

***

Downtown Philly

Barry was in his condo, letting his phone charge, while Elina took a shower, getting ready to go out to eat.

Later, Barry had to set up a get-together with Sosa for the next shipment. Since his phone was charging, he picked Elina's phone up and dialed Sosa's phone number. When he saw the name "Future Babe" pop up, he thought he was tripping. He dialed Sosa's number again, and the same name popped up.

He wondered why Elina had his son's number in her phone under Future Babe. He heard the shower water turn off and put Elina's phone back where he got it from.

"Hey, babe, you ready?" Elina had her body wrapped up in a towel, as she approached him with a kiss.

"Yeah, I'm waiting for you, sexy," Barry said with a smile. One thing he learned was never show your hand too soon.

***

Green County Prison, PA

Gee recently got word that his sister's death was caused at the hand of his own crew, and his boy, Twin.

Never in a million years would he be able to imagine his sister dying at the hands of his own crew, which he had been down with since day one.

Gee was working in the kitchen, on break, thinking about what he was going to do when he touched down. Before he lost his sister, he had plans of going home, getting his CDL license, and working for big time truck companies.

He knew a lot of dudes that left jail with no plan, and came back, or got killed. Now with Shierka dead, someone had to pay for her blood.

Going against the Sosa Gang was like going against family, but they crossed the line.

Sosa Gang

***

South Philly

Traina had been mourning Zels' death at her brother, Twin's crib, all day. Twin was grieving, but his grief was different. He wanted to draw blood to grieve.

"It's ok, sis."

"No, it's not," she cried.

"Trust me, it is, sis. I'm handling it," Twin assured her.

"When is this gonna stop, Twin? You could be next. Twin you have to stop," she told him, crying on his shoulder.

Traina was overwhelmed about Zels' death because she was going to tell him she was pregnant. Last night, she suffered a miscarriage, and that made her even more emotional.

"Stay here for the night." Twin kissed his sister on the forehead and walked off, leaving to get some air because he had been in the crib all day, comforting Traina.

Losing Zels was a hard pill to swallow, but what was even harder to swallow was one of Sin's homies, a little rap nigga, made a rap video last night, dissing Zels and the gang on the internet

Sin's rap homie was throwing a big party out in Chester, so Twin and a few goons planned to slide on the rapper and make a movie out of him.

Romell Tukes

Chapter 47

West Philly

Roddy stopped at a red light, on his way to drop off two keys of coke, which he had in the truck, in his stash spot, under the floor.

Dealing with Sosa Gang had its benefits, and that was more money, more problems

Sosa and Lil Hak dropped forty keys of good product for him and his crew. Roddy never saw that many keys in his life. He felt like the king of Philly.

The light turned green, but the car in front of him wasn't moving. It was ten at night, and Roddy had a lot to do, so he didn't have time for games.

Beep. Beep. Beep. Beep. Beep.

Tat. Tat. Tat. Tat. Tat. Tat. Tat. Tat. Tat. Tat. Tat. Tat. Tat. Tat. Tat. Tat.

Over thirty-six bullets hit the BMW truck, hitting Roddy seven times, before the Outlaws niggas jumped back in the truck to pull off.

***

Southwest Philly

Crispy and his goons parked the rental truck they used to do a hit on tonight. He knew Roddy was out of the picture now, so the D.C. boys were the least of his worries.

"Y'all did good. We gotta go and hit a few clubs up tonight," Crispy said, climbing out of the GMC SUV.

"We smoked that nigga, ock. Better believe it, bull," G-Lay said, getting out on the block to see it was empty because there was a big party across town everybody went to.

"I'ma go check on the stash," Crispy said, about to walk up the stairs into the building, until gunmen with assault rifles rushed out.

Gunmen came from everywhere, behind cars, buildings, and from a park across the street, fifty deep, with all types of big as assault rifles.

"You had a good run," Sosa said, with Lil Hak on his side, as they all surrounded Crispy and his crew.

"In respect to the game," Crispy said, ready to meet his faith. Tat. Tat. Tat. Tat. Tat. Tat. Tat. Tat. Tat.

Bullets went off from every direction, as they took out the niggas Crispy had with him.

The police bent the corner with their lights off because they heard the gun fire, while driving around.

Everybody from Sosa Gang ran, except Sosa and Lil Hak, who fired rounds at both cop cars with their AR-15 assault rifles.

Lil Hak gave one of the cops two headshots, killing him.

Sosa and Lil Hak took off up the block, where their dirt bikes awaited them. Neither of the cop cars moved because one of the cops was injured badly from the bullets Sosa threw at him. The other cop was dead, with his head slumped on the steering wheel.

***

Uptown Philly

Barry walked into a Hala food store he owed, but he'd let a Muslim family from Africa run it for years.

"As-Salaam-Alaikum," Barry said to the big African man, standing at the counter, cutting some Hala chicken.

"Wa-Alaikum-Salaam," the man said.

"You good, brother?"

"Yeah, but did you happen to come out last night?" the African man asked, as he stopped doing what he was doing.

"No, why?" Barry's face said so many words.

"The front door was unlocked this morning, when we opened up," he said.

Barry rushed to the back, where he kept his drugs and money. The African didn't know about the drugs and money he had stashed there, in the back frozen area.

Barry went into the freezer. He had a secret door with a special lock, which he only had the key for. The lock was knocked off, and his worst fear had happened.

He opened the door to see the room that was once filled with tons of coke and money was empty. The room was the same size as a jail cell. He was hurt about it because somebody got over one million dollars in cash.

***

North Philly

Kilow was working his graveyard shift, overnight, dolo tonight. The local police were all on bullshit, since one of their fellow officers got killed, and one was in a coma.

Today was pay day for him in the North Philly section, and hustlers had to pay up.

Kilow pulled up to a side block that was a little dark. He was waiting for a hustler named Max, who'd just started moving birds.

Fog lights pulled up and blinded him, before the lights went off and a man in a hoodie hopped out. He did not have the same body frame or height as Max, but Kilow was high on coke, so he thought he was bugging.

Kilow got out of the car. He wondered where his payment was because Max looked empty handed.

Getting closer to the man in the hoodie, he realized it wasn't Max. But before he could react, it was too late.

Bloc. Bloc. Bloc. Bloc.

Bullets hit Kilow in his forehead and eyes, dropping him.

The man walked off, climbing into the Porsche, and swerving off, listening to old school Nas. The last time he was outside a prison, over twenty years ago, Nas was the hardest lyricist out.

OG Kane hadn't been home but for a few months, and he'd been trying to take back what he left. He was sentenced to life in the FEDS, but he gave back his time on an appeal.

Since coming home, he had been having foot soldiers, like Max, move work for him. So, when Max said Officer Kilow was trying to extort him, OG Kane knew Kilow was going to be a problem.

OG Kane grew up in South Philly and North Philly. He had a strong crew back in the day, and they went by the name Outlaw.

He was one of the main members, besides a few others, and he was back to take over. First, he had to pay someone a visit, and he was on his way there now.

A few blocks away, on 54th Street, Sin was laying low at some fat bitch's crib. The news of Crispy's death took a lot out of him. And hearing cops were killed made it hot outside.

Police were on bullshit, and Sin was riding around with a Draco and a Newood grain Choppa. He'd rather get caught with it than to get caught lacking in Philly.

"I'll be back later," Sin yelled, getting up to leave because he had been stuck in the crib all week, with a fat bitch.

"Byeeee. Go to them bitches house and eat they shit up," the woman yelled from the kitchen, eating a chicken sandwich as a snack.

When Sin opened the door, he saw OG Kane standing there, smiling.

"Who the fuck are you?" Sin asked, seeing the gun in the man's hand.

"A messenger," OG Kane said as the fat bitch peeked her big head out of the kitchen doorway, only to regret it.

BLOC. BLOC. BLOC. BLOC. BLOC. BLOC.
BLOC. BLOC. BLOC. BLOC. BLOC. BLOC.

OG Kane killed both of them, before he walked off to his car, making future plans to take back over his city. But first, he needed his crew. The original Outlaws, who all lived different lifestyles now, besides his daughter, Foxy, who was an active member, but she kept it a secret for years. Now she would have no choice because things were about to change.

Sosa Gang

To Be Continued
Sosa Gang 2
Coming Soon

Lock Down Publications and Ca$h Presents assisted publishing packages.

BASIC PACKAGE $499
Editing
Cover Design
Formatting

UPGRADED PACKAGE $800
Typing
Editing
Cover Design
Formatting

ADVANCE PACKAGE $1,200
Typing
Editing
Cover Design
Formatting
Copyright registration
Proofreading
Upload book to Amazon

LDP SUPREME PACKAGE $1,500
Typing
Editing
Cover Design
Formatting
Copyright registration
Proofreading
Set up Amazon account
Upload book to Amazon
Advertise on LDP Amazon and Facebook page

***Other services available upon request. Additional charges
may apply
Lock Down Publications
P.O. Box 944
Stockbridge, GA 30281-9998
Phone # 470 303-9761

Submission Guideline

Submit the first three chapters of your completed manuscript to ldpsubmissions@gmail.com, subject line: Your book's title. The manuscript must be in a .doc file and sent as an attachment. Document should be in Times New Roman, double spaced and in size 12 font. Also, provide your synopsis and full contact information. If sending multiple submissions, they must each be in a separate email.

Have a story but no way to send it electronically? You can still submit to LDP/Ca$h Presents. Send in the first three chapters, written or typed, of your completed manuscript to:

LDP: Submissions Dept
Po Box 944
Stockbridge, Ga 30281

DO NOT send original manuscript. Must be a duplicate.

Provide your synopsis and a cover letter containing your full contact information.

Thanks for considering LDP and Ca$h Presents.

<u>NEW RELEASES</u>

THE COCAINE PRINCESS 6 by KING RIO

VICIOUS LOYALTY 3 by KINGPEN

SOUL OF A HUSTLER, HEART OF A KILLER 2 by SAYNO-MORE

SOSA GANG by ROMELL TUKES

Romell Tukes

<u>**Coming Soon from Lock Down Publications/Ca$h Presents**</u>

BLOOD OF A BOSS **VI**

SHADOWS OF THE GAME II

TRAP BASTARD II

By **Askari**

LOYAL TO THE GAME **IV**

By **T.J. & Jelissa**

TRUE SAVAGE **VIII**

MIDNIGHT CARTEL IV

DOPE BOY MAGIC IV

CITY OF KINGZ III

NIGHTMARE ON SILENT AVE II

THE PLUG OF LIL MEXICO II

CLASSIC CITY II

By **Chris Green**

BLAST FOR ME **III**

A SAVAGE DOPEBOY III

CUTTHROAT MAFIA III

DUFFLE BAG CARTEL VII

HEARTLESS GOON VI

By **Ghost**

A HUSTLER'S DECEIT III

KILL ZONE II

BAE BELONGS TO ME III

TIL DEATH II

By **Aryanna**

KING OF THE TRAP III

By **T.J. Edwards**

GORILLAZ IN THE BAY V

3X KRAZY III

Sosa Gang

STRAIGHT BEAST MODE III

De'Kari

KINGPIN KILLAZ IV

STREET KINGS III

PAID IN BLOOD III

CARTEL KILLAZ IV

DOPE GODS III

Hood Rich

SINS OF A HUSTLA II

ASAD

YAYO V

Bred In The Game 2

S. Allen

THE STREETS WILL TALK II

By Yolanda Moore

SON OF A DOPE FIEND III

HEAVEN GOT A GHETTO II

SKI MASK MONEY II

By Renta

LOYALTY AIN'T PROMISED III

By Keith Williams

I'M NOTHING WITHOUT HIS LOVE II

SINS OF A THUG II

TO THE THUG I LOVED BEFORE II

IN A HUSTLER I TRUST II

By Monet Dragun

QUIET MONEY IV

EXTENDED CLIP III

THUG LIFE IV

By **Trai'Quan**

Romell Tukes

THE STREETS MADE ME IV
By **Larry D. Wright**
IF YOU CROSS ME ONCE III
ANGEL V
By **Anthony Fields**
THE STREETS WILL NEVER CLOSE IV
By **K'ajji**
HARD AND RUTHLESS III
KILLA KOUNTY IV
By **Khufu**
MONEY GAME III
By **Smoove Dolla**
JACK BOYS VS DOPE BOYS IV
A GANGSTA'S QUR'AN V
COKE GIRLZ II
COKE BOYS II
LIFE OF A SAVAGE V
CHI'RAQ GANGSTAS V
SOSA GANG II
By **Romell Tukes**
MURDA WAS THE CASE III
Elijah R. Freeman
THE STREETS NEVER LET GO III
By **Robert Baptiste**
AN UNFORESEEN LOVE IV
BABY, I'M WINTERTIME COLD III
By **Meesha**

QUEEN OF THE ZOO III
By **Black Migo**

Sosa Gang

A GANGSTA'S PAIN III

By J-Blunt

CONFESSIONS OF A JACKBOY III

By Nicholas Lock

GRIMEY WAYS III

By Ray Vinci

KING KILLA II

By Vincent "Vitto" Holloway

BETRAYAL OF A THUG III

By Fre$h

THE MURDER QUEENS III

By Michael Gallon

THE BIRTH OF A GANGSTER III

By Delmont Player

TREAL LOVE II

By Le'Monica Jackson

FOR THE LOVE OF BLOOD III

By Jamel Mitchell

RAN OFF ON DA PLUG II

By Paper Boi Rari

HOOD CONSIGLIERE III

By Keese

PRETTY GIRLS DO NASTY THINGS II

By Nicole Goosby

PROTÉGÉ OF A LEGEND II

By Corey Robinson

IT'S JUST ME AND YOU II

By Ah'Million

BORN IN THE GRAVE III

By Self Made Tay

FOREVER GANGSTA III
By Adrian Dulan
GORILLAZ IN THE TRENCHES II
By SayNoMore
THE COCAINE PRINCESS VII
By King Rio
CRIME BOSS II
Playa Ray
LOYALTY IS EVERYTHING III
Molotti
HERE TODAY GONE TOMORROW II
By Fly Rock
REAL G'S MOVE IN SILENCE II
By Von Diesel

Available Now

RESTRAINING ORDER **I & II**
By **CA$H & Coffee**
LOVE KNOWS NO BOUNDARIES **I II & III**
By **Coffee**
RAISED AS A GOON I, II, III & IV
BRED BY THE SLUMS I, II, III
BLAST FOR ME I & II
ROTTEN TO THE CORE I II III
A BRONX TALE I, II, III
DUFFLE BAG CARTEL I II III IV V VI

Sosa Gang

HEARTLESS GOON I II III IV V
A SAVAGE DOPEBOY I II
DRUG LORDS I II III
CUTTHROAT MAFIA I II
KING OF THE TRENCHES
By **Ghost**
LAY IT DOWN **I & II**
LAST OF A DYING BREED I II
BLOOD STAINS OF A SHOTTA I & II III
By **Jamaica**
LOYAL TO THE GAME I II III
LIFE OF SIN I, II III
By **TJ & Jelissa**
BLOODY COMMAS I & II
SKI MASK CARTEL I II & III
KING OF NEW YORK I II,III IV V
RISE TO POWER I II III
COKE KINGS I II III IV V
BORN HEARTLESS I II III IV
KING OF THE TRAP I II
By **T.J. Edwards**
IF LOVING HIM IS WRONG…I & II
LOVE ME EVEN WHEN IT HURTS I II III
By **Jelissa**
WHEN THE STREETS CLAP BACK I & II III
THE HEART OF A SAVAGE I II III IV
MONEY MAFIA I II
LOYAL TO THE SOIL I II III
By **Jibril Williams**
A DISTINGUISHED THUG STOLE MY HEART I II & III

241

Romell Tukes

LOVE SHOULDN'T HURT I II III IV

RENEGADE BOYS I II III IV

PAID IN KARMA I II III

SAVAGE STORMS I II III

AN UNFORESEEN LOVE I II III

BABY, I'M WINTERTIME COLD I II

By **Meesha**

A GANGSTER'S CODE I &, II III

A GANGSTER'S SYN I II III

THE SAVAGE LIFE I II III

CHAINED TO THE STREETS I II III

BLOOD ON THE MONEY I II III

A GANGSTA'S PAIN I II

By J-Blunt

PUSH IT TO THE LIMIT

By **Bre' Hayes**

BLOOD OF A BOSS **I, II, III, IV, V**

SHADOWS OF THE GAME

TRAP BASTARD

By **Askari**

THE STREETS BLEED MURDER **I, II & III**

THE HEART OF A GANGSTA I II& III

By **Jerry Jackson**

CUM FOR ME I II III IV V VI VII VIII

An **LDP Erotica Collaboration**

BRIDE OF A HUSTLA **I II & II**

THE FETTI GIRLS **I, II& III**

CORRUPTED BY A GANGSTA I, II III, IV

BLINDED BY HIS LOVE

THE PRICE YOU PAY FOR LOVE I, II ,III

Sosa Gang

DOPE GIRL MAGIC I II III

By **Destiny Skai**

WHEN A GOOD GIRL GOES BAD

By **Adrienne**

THE COST OF LOYALTY I II III

By Kweli

A GANGSTER'S REVENGE **I II III & IV**

THE BOSS MAN'S DAUGHTERS I II III IV V

A SAVAGE LOVE **I & II**

BAE BELONGS TO ME I II

A HUSTLER'S DECEIT I, II, III

WHAT BAD BITCHES DO I, II, III

SOUL OF A MONSTER I II III

KILL ZONE

A DOPE BOY'S QUEEN I II III

TIL DEATH

By **Aryanna**

A KINGPIN'S AMBITON

A KINGPIN'S AMBITION **II**

I MURDER FOR THE DOUGH

By **Ambitious**

TRUE SAVAGE I II III IV V VI VII

DOPE BOY MAGIC I, II, III

MIDNIGHT CARTEL I II III

CITY OF KINGZ I II

NIGHTMARE ON SILENT AVE

THE PLUG OF LIL MEXICO II

CLASSIC CITY

By **Chris Green**

A DOPEBOY'S PRAYER

Romell Tukes

By **Eddie "Wolf" Lee**
THE KING CARTEL **I, II & III**
By **Frank Gresham**
THESE NIGGAS AIN'T LOYAL **I, II & III**
By **Nikki Tee**
GANGSTA SHYT **I II &III**
By **CATO**
THE ULTIMATE BETRAYAL
By **Phoenix**
BOSS'N UP **I , II & III**
By **Royal Nicole**
I LOVE YOU TO DEATH
By **Destiny J**
I RIDE FOR MY HITTA
I STILL RIDE FOR MY HITTA
By **Misty Holt**
LOVE & CHASIN' PAPER
By **Qay Crockett**
TO DIE IN VAIN
SINS OF A HUSTLA
By **ASAD**
BROOKLYN HUSTLAZ
By **Boogsy Morina**
BROOKLYN ON LOCK I & II
By **Sonovia**
GANGSTA CITY
By **Teddy Duke**
A DRUG KING AND HIS DIAMOND I & II III
A DOPEMAN'S RICHES
HER MAN, MINE'S TOO I, II

244

Sosa Gang

CASH MONEY HO'S

THE WIFEY I USED TO BE I II

PRETTY GIRLS DO NASTY THINGS

By Nicole Goosby

TRAPHOUSE KING **I II & III**

KINGPIN KILLAZ I II III

STREET KINGS I II

PAID IN BLOOD **I II**

CARTEL KILLAZ I II III

DOPE GODS I II

By **Hood Rich**

LIPSTICK KILLAH **I, II, III**

CRIME OF PASSION I II & III

FRIEND OR FOE I II III

By **Mimi**

STEADY MOBBN' **I, II, III**

THE STREETS STAINED MY SOUL I II III

By **Marcellus Allen**

WHO SHOT YA **I, II, III**

SON OF A DOPE FIEND I II

HEAVEN GOT A GHETTO

SKI MASK MONEY

Renta

GORILLAZ IN THE BAY **I II III IV**

TEARS OF A GANGSTA I II

3X KRAZY I II

STRAIGHT BEAST MODE I II

DE'KARI

TRIGGADALE I II III

MURDAROBER WAS THE CASE I II

245

Romell Tukes

Elijah R. Freeman
GOD BLESS THE TRAPPERS I, II, III
THESE SCANDALOUS STREETS I, II, III
FEAR MY GANGSTA I, II, III IV, V
THESE STREETS DON'T LOVE NOBODY I, II
BURY ME A G I, II, III, IV, V
A GANGSTA'S EMPIRE I, II, III, IV
THE DOPEMAN'S BODYGAURD I II
THE REALEST KILLAZ I II III
THE LAST OF THE OGS I II III
Tranay Adams
THE STREETS ARE CALLING
Duquie Wilson
MARRIED TO A BOSS I II III
By Destiny Skai & Chris Green
KINGZ OF THE GAME I II III IV V VI
CRIME BOSS
Playa Ray
SLAUGHTER GANG I II III
RUTHLESS HEART I II III
By Willie Slaughter
FUK SHYT
By Blakk Diamond
DON'T F#CK WITH MY HEART I II
By Linnea
ADDICTED TO THE DRAMA I II III
IN THE ARM OF HIS BOSS II
By Jamila
YAYO I II III IV
A SHOOTER'S AMBITION I II

Sosa Gang

BRED IN THE GAME
By S. Allen
TRAP GOD I II III
RICH $AVAGE I II III
MONEY IN THE GRAVE I II III
By Martell Troublesome Bolden
FOREVER GANGSTA I II
GLOCKS ON SATIN SHEETS I II
By Adrian Dulan
TOE TAGZ I II III IV
LEVELS TO THIS SHYT I II
IT'S JUST ME AND YOU
By Ah'Million
KINGPIN DREAMS I II III
RAN OFF ON DA PLUG
By Paper Boi Rari
CONFESSIONS OF A GANGSTA I II III IV
CONFESSIONS OF A JACKBOY I II
By Nicholas Lock
I'M NOTHING WITHOUT HIS LOVE
SINS OF A THUG
TO THE THUG I LOVED BEFORE
A GANGSTA SAVED XMAS
IN A HUSTLER I TRUST
By Monet Dragun
CAUGHT UP IN THE LIFE I II III
THE STREETS NEVER LET GO I II
By Robert Baptiste
NEW TO THE GAME I II III
MONEY, MURDER & MEMORIES I II III

Romell Tukes

By **Malik D. Rice**
LIFE OF A SAVAGE I II III IV
A GANGSTA'S QUR'AN I II III IV
MURDA SEASON I II III
GANGLAND CARTEL I II III
CHI'RAQ GANGSTAS I II III IV
KILLERS ON ELM STREET I II III
JACK BOYZ N DA BRONX I II III
A DOPEBOY'S DREAM I II III
JACK BOYS VS DOPE BOYS I II III
COKE GIRLZ
COKE BOYS
SOSA GANG
By **Romell Tukes**
LOYALTY AIN'T PROMISED I II
By **Keith Williams**
QUIET MONEY I II III
THUG LIFE I II III
EXTENDED CLIP I II
A GANGSTA'S PARADISE
By **Trai'Quan**
THE STREETS MADE ME I II III
By **Larry D. Wright**
THE ULTIMATE SACRIFICE I, II, III, IV, V, VI
KHADIFI
IF YOU CROSS ME ONCE I II
ANGEL I II III IV
IN THE BLINK OF AN EYE
By **Anthony Fields**
THE LIFE OF A HOOD STAR

248

Sosa Gang

By Ca$h & Rashia Wilson

THE STREETS WILL NEVER CLOSE I II III

By K'ajji

CREAM I II III

THE STREETS WILL TALK

By Yolanda Moore

NIGHTMARES OF A HUSTLA I II III

By King Dream

CONCRETE KILLA I II III

VICIOUS LOYALTY I II III

By Kingpen

HARD AND RUTHLESS I II

MOB TOWN 251

THE BILLIONAIRE BENTLEYS I II III

REAL G'S MOVE IN SILENCE

By Von Diesel

GHOST MOB

Stilloan Robinson

MOB TIES I II III IV V VI

SOUL OF A HUSTLER, HEART OF A KILLER I II

GORILLAZ IN THE TRENCHES

By SayNoMore

BODYMORE MURDERLAND I II III

THE BIRTH OF A GANGSTER I II

By Delmont Player

FOR THE LOVE OF A BOSS

By C. D. Blue

MOBBED UP I II III IV

THE BRICK MAN I II III IV V

THE COCAINE PRINCESS I II III IV V VI

Romell Tukes

By King Rio
KILLA KOUNTY I II III IV
By Khufu
MONEY GAME I II
By Smoove Dolla
A GANGSTA'S KARMA I II III
By FLAME
KING OF THE TRENCHES I II III
by **GHOST & TRANAY ADAMS**
QUEEN OF THE ZOO I II
By **Black Migo**
GRIMEY WAYS I II
By Ray Vinci
XMAS WITH AN ATL SHOOTER
By Ca$h & Destiny Skai
KING KILLA
By Vincent "Vitto" Holloway
BETRAYAL OF A THUG I II
By Fre$h
THE MURDER QUEENS I II
By Michael Gallon
TREAL LOVE
By Le'Monica Jackson
FOR THE LOVE OF BLOOD I II
By Jamel Mitchell
HOOD CONSIGLIERE I II
By Keese
PROTÉGÉ OF A LEGEND
By Corey Robinson
BORN IN THE GRAVE I II

Sosa Gang

By Self Made Tay

MOAN IN MY MOUTH

By XTASY

TORN BETWEEN A GANGSTER AND A GENTLEMAN

By J-BLUNT & Miss Kim

LOYALTY IS EVERYTHING I II

Molotti

HERE TODAY GONE TOMORROW

By Fly Rock

PILLOW PRINCESS

By S. Hawkins

<u>BOOKS BY LDP'S CEO, CA$H</u>

TRUST IN NO MAN

TRUST IN NO MAN 2

TRUST IN NO MAN 3

BONDED BY BLOOD

SHORTY GOT A THUG

THUGS CRY

THUGS CRY 2

THUGS CRY 3

TRUST NO BITCH

TRUST NO BITCH 2

TRUST NO BITCH 3

TIL MY CASKET DROPS

RESTRAINING ORDER

RESTRAINING ORDER 2

IN LOVE WITH A CONVICT

LIFE OF A HOOD STAR

XMAS WITH AN ATL SHOOTER

Sosa Gang